TIANA

Disney PRINCESS

TALES of Courage AND Kindness

WRITTEN BY

Aubre Andrus
Sudipta Bardhan-Quallen
Marie Chow
Erin Falligant
Suzanne Francis
Eric Geron
Kalikolehua Hurley
Kelly Starling Lyons
Kathy McCullough
Kitty Richards
Elizabeth Rudnick

ILLUSTRATED BY

Nabi H. Ali
Nicoletta Baldari
Liam Brazier
Alina Chau
Nathanna Érica
Sara Kipin
Ann Marcellino
Tara N. Whitaker
Alice X. Zhang
Studio IBOIX

COVER ART BY

Kate Forrester

DISNEP PRESS

LOS ANGELES • NEW YORK

CONTENTS

Tiana is a visionary who learned from her father the joy of sharing good food with others. She believes the only way to get what you want in this world is through hard work. She is focused and driven to achieve her goals. But when she was accidentally turned into a frog, Tiana learned that love is just as important as hard work. Now, as a princess, Tiana lives with her husband, Prince Naveen, and runs her very own restaurant, Tiana's Palace.

DADDY'S FRONT PORCH

WRITTEN BY KELLY STARLING LYONS & ILLUSTRATED BY TARA N. WHITAKER

Princess Tiana walked onto the rooftop of her restaurant and gazed at Evangeline, the Evening Star, shimmering in the satin sky. When she was little, her daddy told her to believe in the power of wishing but to always remember to put effort into making her dream come true.

"Isn't she beautiful?" Tiana said as her husband, Prince Naveen, joined her.

"Yes," he said, looking into Tiana's eyes. "She is."

Tiana smiled at Naveen. She wished her daddy could have met him. He had passed away before so many amazing things happened in her life. She still couldn't believe she had been turned into a frog, married Naveen, and become a princess. And then there was the restaurant she'd opened in honor of her father. It had always been her daddy's dream that they would open a restaurant together.

Transforming a beat-up sugar mill into a place for good food and good company was a vision that had passed from his heart to hers. Naveen had helped her change that falling-apart building into Tiana's Palace, known for miles around. People lined up to get a taste of her daddy's famous gumbo and her mouthwatering beignets. He would have been so proud.

Tiana had been thinking a lot about her daddy, like she did every year around his birthday.

TIANA IS . . .

AMBITIOUS

HOPEFUL

SELF-RELIANT

FOCUSED

RESILIENT

HARDWORKING

TIANA'S DREAM:

To open her own restaurant

HEROIC MOMENT:

Braving the bayou to break the shadow man's curse

SIDEKICK:

Ray

FAMOUS QUOTE:

"The only way to get what you want in this world is through hard work."

"I want to do something extra special to honor Daddy this year," she said.

"Achidanza!" Naveen said in his native Maldonian. "That's a great idea. Count on me to help out."

But what should she do?

The next morning, Tiana was on a mission. When she set her mind to something, watch out. Her daddy's birthday was only a week away. She had to come up with something just right.

Tiana knew exactly where to go first—to visit her mama, Eudora. As she entered her childhood home, Tiana marveled at the ruby gown her mom was making. In her hands, tulle, lace, and ribbons were more powerful than a magic wand. She was the best seamstress in all of New Orleans.

"Mama," Tiana said, kissing her on the cheek, "you outdid

yourself. The First Lady and the queen of Maldonia would be jealous."

"Aw, thank you, honey," she said. "But you didn't come all this way to compliment this dress. What's on your mind?"

Tiana picked up the picture of her daddy in his Army uniform that sat on her mom's table. His distinguished service cross for heroism during the Great War lay nearby.

"Daddy's birthday is coming up. I want to do something that shows people who he was."

"You honor him and me every day," her mother said, "by just being you."

"I know, Mama," she said, "but I *want* to do something. You remember how Daddy used to give *us* presents on his birthday. He would insist on making gumbo and inviting everyone over to share. We would eat on the front porch and laugh. He gave to others all his life. He deserves a tribute to him."

"Yes, your father—James—was a good man. I won't try to talk you out of it. Lord knows you're hardheaded just like him," she said, chuckling. "You won't stop until you make it happen."

Tiana left her mom's feeling good, but just as unsure about what to do. On her way back to her restaurant, she saw a man and a woman who were asking people for money to buy lunch. Their faces were pale. Their clothes were old and torn. It hurt Tiana that they were hungry. Her daddy had always said a pot of gumbo does more than fill your stomach; it fills your heart with love.

"I'm Tiana," she said. "What are your names?"

"I'm Fleur," the woman said, "and this is my husband, Jean. We fell on hard times and could use a little help getting back up."

"Y'all come on into the Palace," Tiana said, "and get something to eat. Don't worry about paying. The meal is on me."

They looked at each other like they weren't sure she was serious. Then they followed her inside. Their eyes bugged as they took in the arched ceiling and grand chandelier. They stared up at the skylight and gaped at the intricate designs of the wrought-iron balconies. They admired the tables covered with linens that looked like lily pads.

"Make sure Fleur and Jean get whatever they want," Tiana told Naveen, who welcomed everyone as they arrived.

She winked at them.

Ever since Tiana had opened her restaurant, she'd made sure to look out for people who didn't have as much as she did. If someone wanted to eat, she would accept whatever they could pay and give out food for free to those who couldn't.

"Tia!" called her best friend, Charlotte LaBouff, as Tiana entered the main dining room. "Tia, didn't you hear me?"

"Sorry, Lottie," she said, giving her a hug. "I guess I was lost in my thoughts. I want to do something special to honor Daddy, but I don't know what to do."

They sat together at a table. Charlotte stared into space like she was thinking through options.

"I know, I know!" Lottie squealed, and took Tiana's hands in hers. "A celebration! My father loves those. That would be a great way to honor the memory of your daddy. Let's have a ball and name it after him."

While Lottie chattered about silk gowns, dances, and fine china, Tiana thought about Daddy. He had loved bringing people together, but he didn't care about fanciness. He liked simplicity and sincerity more than fuss.

"Can't you see it, Tia?" she said. "Tia?"

Tiana noticed a man peering into the front window of her restaurant. Something about him looked familiar. Where did she know him from?

"Sorry, Lottie," she said, standing up and heading to the door. "I'll be right back."

"Excuse me, sir," she said, once outside. "Do I know you?"

"Are you Miss Tiana?" he asked. "I heard that James's little girl opened a restaurant. I had to come see it for myself."

"You knew my daddy?" she asked with wide eyes.

"Sure did. Your daddy was something special," he said. "I was in the war with him. He would give anyone the shirt off his back and laid down his life to keep others safe."

As her eyes brimmed with tears, Tiana smiled. That was her daddy. And she remembered who this was—Mr. Larkin, the friend of her father's she'd seen in so many pictures.

"Wasn't easy," he said. "Just like now, some people only cared about the color of our skin. They didn't see us as heroes. But your daddy stood up for anyone who needed it."

Tiana thought about that. She and Lottie were best friends, but not everybody liked that. Her restaurant was a magical place where all people could be together, but at most places, Black and white people had to be separate. That was the law. Tiana hoped for a day when segregation and injustice would end. She wanted everyone to be treated equally, not just at her restaurant but everywhere.

"Won't you come inside?" she said. "I'd love to show you around."

"Not today," he said. "But it sure is good to see you. James talked so much about his wife and little daughter who had a gift that gleamed brighter than a star. Feel like I already know you."

Tiana thought about what Mr. Larkin had said as she walked back inside.

"Who was that, Tia?" Charlotte asked.

"A friend of my daddy's," replied Tiana.

"That's nice," Charlotte said. "Now what do you think about the ball?"

"I don't know, Lottie," Tiana said, sighing. "Daddy was humble. Not sure that fits who he was."

Just then Louis, the star of the band Firefly Five Plus Lou, came over.

"Hey, Tiana and Charlotte," he said, flashing his toothy smile. Newcomers to Tiana's Palace were always startled to see an alligator playing trumpet. But once he started to swing, they forgot all about that as toe tapping and finger snapping took over. "Y'all want to hear what I'm working on?"

"Of course," Tiana said.

His tail bouncing as he bopped, their friend played a solo that would put Louis Armstrong to shame. Lottie cheered and clapped. Tiana stood and gave the big alligator a hug.

"Amazing," she said. "I'm trying to think of something special for my daddy's birthday. Got any ideas?"

"Your daddy liked jazz, right?" Louis said. "How about a jam session in his name? The guys and I could play something special."

"Did someone say 'jam'?" Naveen said, walking up while strumming a ukulele. "Don't forget about me."

Tiana smiled. Her daddy had loved music. Having Louis and Naveen play in his honor would be special. Maybe that could be it.

"Thanks," she said. "I need to think it through."

She hugged Lottie goodbye and headed to her cozy office. That's where she came up with new recipes and made plans for the future. She stared at the poster her daddy had created for the restaurant he hoped they'd open. She remembered when it was just a twinkle in his eyes.

She wrote down the ideas her friends had shared for his birthday celebration—a ball, a concert. Did those show who her daddy was?

Before she knew it, evening covered the French Quarter like a blanket. It was time to get ready for bed. In her room, Tiana paced, her mind still racing. She needed some air. She walked up to the rooftop, the city of New Orleans sparkling below her. She stared again at Evangeline, glittering like a beacon. Next to Evangeline was her dear friend Ray's star. Tiana closed her eyes and made a wish.

"Please help me think of something special for Daddy's birthday," she said.

Tiana opened her eyes and took a long last look at the twinkling stars before returning to her room and turning in. No sooner had she fallen asleep than a flickering light appeared, waking her.

"Naveen," she called sleepily. "Did you leave the light on?"

"You got a light inside, cher," someone said. "You just got to let it lead you."

Tiana sat up straight. She knew that voice. She looked around and saw Ray, her firefly friend from the bayou, circling her head. She loved seeing his face again.

"Me and Evangeline heard your wish. But you got all you need right there," he said, landing near her heart and shining bright.

Tiana thought about her daddy saying that good food brings people together. It makes their hearts glow just like Ray was showing her. She could almost hear his voice telling her to never forget what's most important.

When she woke up the next morning, she realized Ray hadn't really visited her. It had all been a dream. But a name blazed in her head like a sign trimmed with lights—*Daddy's Front Porch*. That had been a place full of love and laughter. She remembered how a pot of gumbo and a place to gather had brought everyone together in hard times and good. No one had gone without food when her daddy was around.

She had her idea. It would be a lot of work. Tiana would need everyone to pitch in, but they could do it. She hopped out of bed, ready for the challenge. Tiana could already see her dream taking shape.

Along with being the best seamstress around, Eudora was the manager of Tiana's Palace. Tiana couldn't wait to tell her the news.

"Mama," she said when she saw her,

"I know how to HONOR Daddy."

Her mother stretched out her arms and wrapped her in a hug. "That doesn't surprise me one bit."

Tiana filled in her mama and Naveen. Then she asked Lottie, Louis, and members of her staff to come to a planning meeting at the restaurant. She looked at everyone gathered at the tables and smiled. Bringing people together was what her daddy had been all about. Having them help with the tribute would celebrate who he was.

"Thanks, y'all, for being here," Tiana said. "My daddy had a heart for helping whoever needed it. That's the spirit I want to show on his birthday. We're gonna open our doors each week and invite everyone to eat for free. I'm gonna call it Daddy's Front Porch."

Tiana's Palace didn't have a front porch like her childhood home. But Tiana knew how to re-create the feeling. People could walk right in, no reservation needed, no bill to pay. Laughter would ring as forks and spoons sang. Riffs of friendship would float in the air. And Daddy's Front Porch wouldn't just offer food; it would spread hope. If anyone had extra clothes or food, they could share it with others.

As everyone clapped, Tiana's mama nodded and wiped a tear from her eye. Tiana knew how she felt without Eudora saying a word.

"Oh, Tia," Lottie said. "This is just the most special thing I have ever heard. Sign me up for the decorations."

"Me too," Tiana's mother said.

"You know we gotta have music," Louis said, flashing his toothy grin and tapping out a beat with his foot.

"Yeah," Naveen said. "I can help with that."

"The food is the most important part," Tiana said, looking at her chefs.

They promised the dishes would be the best they'd ever made. Tiana beamed. It was all coming together.

On the big day, Tiana could hardly stand still. She paced around the restaurant making sure everything was ready. Her stomach fluttered like the day Tiana's Palace had first opened. She stood in the center of the ballroom and admired the big picture of Daddy that Lottie and Mama had set up near the stage. If only he could be here to see this.

Tiana stepped outside and smiled at the sign whose glowing letters spelled out *Daddy's Front Porch* just like in her dream. But it was missing something. Tiana stared and stared. What did it need? Then it came to her. She raced into the kitchen and got her daddy's gumbo pot. She lined it with paper and put it right by the sign. That would be a way for people to leave donations if they wanted to help others who needed it.

Finally, it was time to start the celebration. She gathered everyone together to thank them for making this happen. Naveen kissed her cheek.

"Everything will be perfect," he said.

Tiana took a breath and beamed her brightest smile. Lottie blew her a kiss.

"Okay, everyone," she said. "Showtime."

Fleur and Jean were the first ones inside. A stream of people flowed in behind them. Old and young, Black and white, some had never been to a place like this. Lights lit up the room like fireflies. After being escorted to their tables, guests were told to order anything they wished. Gumbo, étouffée, beignets—all on the house.

Fleur walked up to Tiana.

"You helped us when we needed it," she said. "Now look at you shining on our whole city. Count on us to pitch in any way you need." Tiana hugged her. This moment was bigger than her or her daddy. It was the start of something magical for the community.

As everyone ate and talked, Louis and Naveen got the joint jumping. Jazz and joy swirled all around. Tiana's mama had never smiled so much.

Tiana sensed someone looking at her and turned around. It was Mr. Larkin.

"You came back," she said, giving him a hug. "Thank you."

"You did good, Tiana," he said. "I know James is proud of you, and so am I."

Her eyes filling with tears, Tiana walked to the stage and tried to find the words to express what was in her heart.

"I want to thank everybody for coming," she said. "Today, we celebrate the life of a man I am honored to call my daddy. He gave a hand to anyone who needed one. We're going to keep his spirit alive. Daddy's Front Porch is going to be once every week, a day when no one pays to eat at Tiana's Palace."

The crowd cheered. Naveen smiled at his wife. Tiana felt something electric race through her heart. Even if she couldn't see him, she knew Daddy was there.

Tiana slipped away to her bedroom to have a moment to herself. Through her window, she saw Evangeline shining in the ebony night and knew she had something to do. Tiana stepped onto the rooftop to say thank you. As she did, another star lit up beside Evangeline. She knew that was Ray. Her heart filled with love.

"Thank you, Evangeline and Ray," she whispered as she closed her eyes.

"Tiana," Naveen said, walking up behind her and putting his hands on her shoulders, "look!"

When she opened her eyes, she saw a third star glowing near the other two. Its brilliance made her think of big dreams and sparkling eyes. Tiana could almost hear a booming laugh and deep voice saying she'd done all right. She wiped away the tear that rolled down her cheek, and smiled.

"Happy birthday, Daddy," Tiana said, laying her head on Naveen's shoulder.

How can you HELP your COMMUNITY?

BELLE

Belle adores reading. Different stories take her to new places, introduce her to new people, and allow her to see new perspectives. She is confident and comfortable being herself. In fact, Belle's mind is one thing she is very sure of, and she is not afraid to share her opinion with anyone. But her status as the town outsider taught her to look past what is on the surface and see the best in people.

NEW FRIENDS

WRITTEN BY KATHY MCCULLOUGH & ILLUSTRATED BY ANN MARCELLINO

Belle relaxed in a nook of the castle library, rereading one of her favorite books. The Prince had gifted her the library when he was still the Beast, and she spent as much time as she could in it, usually with a book on her lap. She was amazed at the way inked symbols on a page could bring a whole story to life. It was magical how letters formed words and words formed sentences that could transport her to other places, teach her about new things, and introduce her to people who seemed so real, it was as if they were right there with her.

The door to the library flew open, and a very real person burst into the room. "Belle! Your father has returned!" cried Monsieur Cogsworth, the castle's majordomo.

Belle hurried down to the castle's grand entranceway. "Welcome home to the castle, Papa!" she said, giving Maurice a warm hug.

"Just a brief stop for the night, sweetheart," Maurice replied, "before I head north." Belle's father spent the spring traveling to festivals and fairs to sell his inventions. "But look what I have for you!" He handed Belle three wrapped packages. "Books from Spain, Portugal . . . and Morocco!"

The castle library had plenty of books on the history and geography of nations other than France, where Belle lived. But while atlases and history books offered facts, Belle believed storybooks could show what the people in those lands were really like—how they

BELLE IS . . .

INTELLIGENT
GENEROUS
A LIFELONG LEARNER
LOYAL
PASSIONATE
AUTHENTICALLY HERSELF

BELLE'S DREAM:

To never stop learning

HEROIC MOMENT:

Sacrificing her freedom to
save her father

SIDEKICK:

Lumiere

FAMOUS QUOTE:

"I want adventure in the great,
wide somewhere."

lived, and what their hopes and dreams were. A few collections of fairy tales and folktales from around the world dotted the castle library's shelves, but Belle longed to have newer stories about these places. When Maurice had set off on his journey the month before, Belle had given him a stack of French books to take along to offer to foreign travelers he met in return for books from their countries.

Belle eagerly unwrapped the top package and opened the first book. "Oh, no . . ." she said. She held up the book to show Maurice. "It's in Spanish. I don't know that language!" Belle shook her head with a laugh. "I should have guessed the books would be in their countries' languages." She flipped through a book from Portugal—which was, of course, in Portuguese. She then opened the first Moroccan book. "This must be Arabic!" she said, marveling at the beautiful cursive letters. "There are wonderful stories on these pages, I know it!" She ran her fingers over the Arabic words. "But they're hidden from me—even though the words are plain to see."

"I searched the whole library," Belle told Maurice and the Prince at dinner that night. "Twice. But we don't have *any* foreign-language dictionaries."

"There are dictionaries that translate French into other languages?" the Prince asked.

"I'm sure there are," Belle said. "But I've never seen one. Those types of dictionaries are probably kept in places like university libraries."

"Oh! That reminds me!" Maurice searched through the many pockets in his vest until he found a small envelope. He handed it to Belle. "I was given this with the books from Morocco."

Belle opened the envelope. Her eyes widened as she read the note inside. "A librarian from a university in Fès, Morocco, is coming *here*!" The librarian's name was Fatima Baddou, and she'd heard about Belle's quest to expand the castle library from the Moroccan merchant who had given Maurice the Arabic books.

"We haven't had guests at the castle since I was a little boy," the Prince said, worried. "I wouldn't know what to do or how to behave."

"You have *so* had a guest since then," Belle reminded him, gesturing to herself. "That turned out pretty well." She smiled.

The Prince blushed. "That was different. That was . . . *you*."

Belle took his hand and squeezed it. "Just be yourself," she said. "Your new friendly self." The Prince laughed.

He wasn't the only occupant of the castle worried about the visit, however. "They're arriving in a week?" Cogsworth exclaimed when he heard the news. "No, no, no. That's too soon!" Cogsworth's job was to make sure everything at the castle ran smoothly. A week would not be *nearly* enough time to get everything ready. "How do we prepare the rooms?" he asked. "Do they prefer tea at bedtime, or warm milk? Do they wake up early, or do they like to sleep in?"

"Exactement!" said Lumiere, the castle maître d'. "We don't know what time they prefer to dine! Are the meals to be big or small? Do they like entertainment *with* their meal, or after—or both?"

Even Mrs. Potts the cook, who was usually so cheerful, clutched her apron nervously. "Oh, dear me! We don't know what kinds of fruits and vegetables they like, or what their favorite desserts might be," she said. "I want them to feel at home—but I have no idea where to begin in choosing which recipes to make!"

"Do we have to learn Moroccan?" asked Chip, Mrs. Potts's young son.

"In Morocco, they speak Arabic," Belle explained to Chip. "Mademoiselle Baddou is bringing an interpreter with her, along with a driver and a cook. The interpreter will be able to translate Arabic into French for us, and vice versa." Belle smiled at the others. "As for the answers to the rest of your questions, I know just where to look."

Belle invited the group to the library and brought out all the books she could find about Morocco. "If you still have questions when the visitors arrive, we'll just ask!"

When the visitors arrived, however, the first questions were for Belle. In the drawing room, as Lina, the interpreter, translated Fatima's words into French, Fatima asked Belle about growing up in the village, and about how she had ended up a princess. Fatima listened, rapt, as Lina translated Belle's answers into Arabic. After Belle finished the story of her adventures in the castle, Fatima responded in a voice filled with awe. "It's like something out of a fairy tale!" Lina said, translating.

Belle smiled in agreement, although she thought Fatima's life sounded even more magical. "To be a librarian at the oldest library in the world!" Belle said. Belle had researched the University of al-Qarawiyyin, where the library had been built centuries before.

"Fatima is named for Fatima al-Fihri, the woman who built the university," Lina said, translating for Fatima. "Because her parents chose this name, she says it was her destiny to grow up to be a librarian there. Luckily, it was her dream, as well!"

> " It's so WONDERFUL to meet someone who LOVES books like I do, "

Belle said. She and Fatima exchanged smiles as Lina repeated Belle's words in Arabic. Belle wished she and Fatima didn't have to wait for their words to be translated. They had so much to talk about!

Fatima spoke again. "Fatima wants to ask you more about your project to expand your library with books from other cultures," Lina said. "This is something they have been doing at al-Qarawiyyin for many years, and translating them as well."

Before Belle could reply, Mrs. Potts and Chip entered with a tea cart. "Moroccan almond briouats," Mrs. Potts said proudly, holding out a tray of triangular pastries.

"Briouat!" Fatima said with a smile. She and Lina each took one of the flaky treats. When they bit into them, however, they both winced and exchanged glances.

"Oh, dear me," Mrs. Potts said. "The book only had a picture—no recipe. So I had to guess what was in it."

Fatima spoke to Lina in Arabic. "Our cook could teach you the recipe, if you like," Lina told Mrs. Potts, translating for Fatima.

"That would be wonderful!" Mrs. Potts replied. She gestured to the tea cart. "In the meantime, we have plenty of bread and jam."

"Mulberry!" Chip said, lifting the jar. He didn't have a good grip on it, however, and it tipped over, spilling thick purple jam onto Lina's lap.

"Sorry!" Chip, near tears, bit his lip.

"It's perfectly fine," Lina reassured him. "I have many lively nephews and nieces—I am used to things getting a little messy now and then. I can go to my room and change." She turned to Fatima and they exchanged a few words in Arabic. Fatima smiled and nodded in response, and Mrs. Potts led Lina off to the guest quarters.

Belle and Fatima were left alone in the drawing room, and the silence between them grew awkward. The guest quarters were at the opposite end of the castle, so Belle expected it would be some time before Lina returned. Knowing Fatima loved books as much as she did, Belle decided they'd both feel more comfortable surrounded by them. She stood and gestured for Fatima to join her. They left the drawing room and made their way through the halls of the castle, exchanging shy smiles. When they passed Cogsworth, Belle asked him to tell Lina where they'd gone.

Finally, they arrived at the castle library. Fatima let out an exclamation of delight and said something in Arabic. Although Belle didn't understand the words, she could tell they were a compliment—then she remembered hearing one of the Arabic words before, during their earlier conversation.

Belle pulled a book off a shelf and held it up. *"Kitab . . . ?"* she asked.

Fatima nodded. "Kitab!"

Belle smiled and handed the book to Fatima. "Book."

"Book," Fatima repeated. She crossed to the shelves. "Kitab, kitab, kitab," she said, tapping the spines of the books. She then gestured toward all the shelves. *"Maktaba!"*

"Maktaba . . ." Belle said. She remembered hearing Fatima say this word earlier, too.

"Al-Qarawiyyin," Fatima said and pointed to herself. "Maktabti." She gestured around the room again. "Maktabat Belle!"

Belle knew al-Qarawiyyin was the library where Fatima worked. And right now they were in Belle's . . .

"Library!" Belle said.

"Library!" Fatima repeated, clapping her hands in delight. She gestured from herself to Belle, and then to the books.

Belle was pretty sure she understood the gesture. "Yes!" she said. "Let's find more words to learn!" Belle gathered several books with

illustrations, to help them teach each other. They then paged through the books, sharing the French and Arabic words for each item.

"*Wardah,*" Fatima said, pointing to a painting of a pink rose.

"Wardah," Belle repeated. "Rose."

"Rose!" Fatima said.

As they continued, Belle learned *qamar* meant "moon" in Arabic, and *fil* meant "elephant." Belle brought out paper and pens so they could draw pictures of items they couldn't find in the books. They acted out movements like walking and sitting down, sharing the words in each language. They made faces to show emotions.

"*Saeeda,*" Fatima said, adopting a joyful smile.

Belle repeated the Arabic as Fatima nodded in approval. "Happy," Belle said, translating the word to French.

"Happy," Fatima said. She and Belle exchanged warm smiles.

It became harder when they attempted more complicated ideas, however. Belle tried to ask Fatima about her journey from Fès to the castle, but Fatima just shook her head, not understanding. Belle opened a map and used her fingers to mime walking from Fès to her village. Fatima replied in Arabic, gesturing with her hands as she spoke, but Belle was unsure what she was saying.

Belle tried to think of another way they could teach each other, something they hadn't yet tried. Her eyes scanned the titles on the shelves for a book that might help them and landed on a collection of folktales. She brought down the book and paged through to a tale from Morocco. She held it out to Fatima.

Fatima took the book and studied the illustrations on the different pages. A smile came over her face as well. "*'Al-Tair Al-Azraq'!*" she said. She flipped back to the first page of the story and pointed at the title, repeating the words.

"'The Blue Bird'!" Belle said. "You know it?" Belle grabbed some paper and drew a blue bird. She showed it to Fatima, who nodded happily.

Together, Belle and Fatima acted out the story, about a princess who was visited every evening by two blue birds. The birds were actually men who had been placed under a spell. The princess developed a fondness for one of the birds, and after the spell was broken, she and the man fell in love.

Belle and Fatima each recited the words in her own language as they went along. They then repeated the passages, with Belle doing her best to match the Arabic words to her actions, and Fatima doing the same with the French words. Their actions grew silly at times, causing them both to dissolve into laughter. When either got something wrong, the other would shake her head, and they'd try again. It was like solving a puzzle, each new word or phrase they learned adding another piece to help bring the bigger picture to life.

After they reached the story's happy ending, Fatima picked up a picture book they'd looked at earlier, about two bears who meet in the woods and become friends. Fatima opened it to the final illustration, of the bears holding hands. *"Asdiqaa,"* she said. She pointed to herself and then to Belle.

"Asdiqaa," Belle repeated. She was pretty sure she understood what the word meant. "Friends," she said.

"Friends," Fatima repeated just as the library door swung open and the Prince entered.

Belle rushed over to him and grabbed his hands. "Fatima and I have been teaching each other our languages!" she told him. "I can't believe how much I've learned!"

"I'm glad things have been going well here," the Prince said, looking grim. "I'm afraid that's not the case in the rest of the castle."

"Why?" Belle asked. "What's happened?"

"It's a disaster!" Cogsworth cried as he raced in behind the Prince, wringing his hands. Lumiere and Mrs. Potts entered next, each talking over the other.

"Calm down!" Belle urged them. "Tell me what happened—one at a time."

Belle soon learned that the attempts by the Prince and the others to communicate with their visitors without an interpreter had not gone as well as it had with Belle and Fatima. The Prince had tried to invite the driver to go riding in the woods but was confused when the driver pointed to himself and then to the horses as he spoke. "He smiled while he was talking," the Prince said. "But then he shook his head! I wasn't sure if he was saying yes—or no."

Fatima's cook had joined Mrs. Potts in the kitchen, where she showed him the picture of the almond briouats. The cook had pointed out the ingredients and the measuring utensils for each, but Mrs. Potts didn't understand his instructions and the result had tasted even worse than her first attempt.

"And I'm afraid it will be *impossible* for me to perform this evening!" Lumiere declared in despair. He explained that the cook and the driver had passed by the room where he had been practicing his evening music selection. He had just finished a cabaret song when they both said something in Arabic. Assuming they preferred a different type of music, Lumiere switched to opera, but they spoke again, using the same words. "I tried many other music styles," Lumiere told Belle. "But they kept saying the same thing. I could not figure out their favorite." Lumiere sighed sadly. "Because the entertainment for guests must be the best or *nothing*"—Lumiere hung his head—"it will have to be nothing."

Belle glanced at Fatima, who had been listening closely. Fatima may not have understood everything that was said, but Belle could tell the librarian had guessed there had been some misunderstandings between the visitors and castle residents. The eyes of the two new friends met, and a message passed between them—they didn't need words or even gestures to understand each other. Fatima nodded and left the room.

"Fatima will find Lina," Belle told the others. "I'm sure we can sort this all out and you can try again."

"But the interpreter can't be everywhere at once!" the Prince said. "I'm worried we'll make our guests' stay worse!"

"I must agree," Cogsworth said.

"I *don't* agree," Belle said. "Fatima and I found a way to understand each other. It wasn't always easy—but we didn't give up. And now we're friends!" She glanced around at the others. "It can be scary to get to know new people—but *all* friends are people you didn't know when you first met them." She shot a meaningful look at the Prince: Belle and he had once been strangers, too.

"I guess it *would* be nicer for us to become friends with our visitors," the Prince admitted. The others nodded.

Fatima entered the library with Lina—now in fresh clothes—followed by the driver and the cook. With Lina's help, the residents and guests worked out their misunderstandings. "The driver thought

you were showing him how to saddle a horse," Lina explained to the Prince. "He was trying to explain that he already knew how." She smiled. "He would be honored to go riding with you." The Prince grinned at the driver, relieved and pleased, and the driver nodded.

Lina turned to Mrs. Potts. "Our cook knows how protective other cooks are of their kitchens, but if you would allow, he could *show* you the steps, and you could make the briouats together."

"Oh, yes! That would be perfect!" said Mrs. Potts, beaming at the cook.

Lina then told Lumiere that the cook and driver were asking him if he would teach them some of his music. "In return, they would love to share their favorite Moroccan songs with you."

"I would be delighted!" Lumiere said, thrilled. "I am always eager to add to my musical repertoire."

By the end of their stay, the visitors and their hosts had become friends. The cook taught Mrs. Potts the true recipe for briouats, and she taught him how to make chocolate croissants. The Prince and the driver explored the land around the castle and translated the names for different horse breeds for each other, using an illustrated book from the library.

After their final dinner together, Lumiere serenaded the group with a selection of his favorite songs, along with the new Moroccan ones he had learned. The guests joined in for these last songs, filling the castle with music.

The next morning, as the visitors got ready to leave, Fatima, with Lina, took Belle aside. Fatima spoke, and Lina translated. "Fatima would love for you to write to each other, and work together on a plan to make more language dictionaries, for libraries everywhere."

"Yes! Definitely!" Belle said. "And I'll come visit *you*. And see *your* library."

Lina translated, and Fatima nodded with enthusiasm. Fatima exchanged whispers with Lina, and then Fatima spoke. "Yes, please visit!" Fatima said in French. "Please visit *soon*!"

"Do you want to take a trip to Morocco?" the Prince asked after the visitors had left.

"What better way to learn Arabic?" Belle said with a grin. "And then we can plan our other travels!"

"*Other* travels?" the Prince said, looking intrigued.

Belle took his hands and smiled up at him. "There are so many lands to visit and people to meet—and languages to study!" she said. "Isn't it wonderful to know we'll never, *ever* run out of new things to learn?"

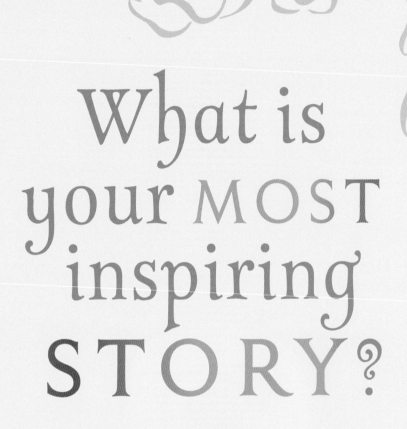

What is your MOST inspiring STORY?

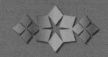

MOANA

Moana is a sea-loving, strong-willed girl. Though she has moments of self-doubt, she has great pride in who she is and does not back away from challenges. She approaches new experiences and tasks with the utmost seriousness and will stand her ground to fight for what she values, even when all seems lost.

THE OCEAN GUARDIANS

WRITTEN BY KALIKOLEHUA HURLEY & ILLUSTRATED BY LIAM BRAZIER

Eight-year-old Moana glided underwater along the amber- and gold-speckled seafloor of Motunui beach, admiring a string of sparkling seashells, when suddenly she came face to face with two large deep-green eyes. Her heart soared—it was Fonu, a sea turtle she had known her whole life. Long ago, when they were both little, Moana had saved Fonu from a few very hungry birds, holding a leaf over the turtle as she scampered across the sand and into the sea. Moana didn't know if Fonu remembered that day. But as she would soon discover, the turtle had never forgotten.

Fonu dove deeper, and Moana followed. There beneath the waves, the water grew quiet and calm—a welcome change to the hustle and bustle on Motunui island, where Moana would one day lead her people as chief. More than anything, Moana loved these moments with her special friend.

Time for a breath! As Moana fluttered up to the surface, a muffled sound tumbled into her ears. *"Moana!"* Her mother, Sina, called her from shore. *"Moana, where are you?"*

Moana pierced through the water's surface. "Right here, Mom!"

"Almost time to come in," Sina said. She pointed to the horizon. "Look at those faraway clouds. What are they telling you?"

Moana treaded water as she studied them, just as Sina had taught her to do, and just as her ancestors had for generations. Signs from nature, like skies, winds, and seas, helped her people predict oncoming weather. "Those clouds are low, dark, and thick . . . and heading our way."

"Which means—"

"Stormy seas are coming."

Sina smiled proudly. Just then, they heard a *chirp!* "Hi, Fonu," Sina greeted the turtle, who popped her head above the waves. "No wonder you were underwater for so long, Moana," Sina said, her eyes twinkling. "Turtles are such special creatures."

"Especially Fonu." Moana beamed.

"I'm glad she has you . . . and that *you* have *her*, too," Sina added softly.

They watched the turtle slip back into the sea.

"One more dive with Fonu, and then we'll leave?" Moana asked.

Sina thought it over. She rubbed her arms as the wind began to gust. "Okay," she agreed. "Just one more. But make it quick."

"I will," Moana promised. She filled her lungs with air and dove back down.

Underwater, large bunches of jade-green seaweed bounced spiritedly on the seafloor. Their seaward direction made Moana pause. She could tell the seaweed was being carried out to the deep by a strong current—one that could very well take her there, too. But only if she wasn't careful.

Just then, Fonu zipped by, chirping merrily as she crunched on beakfuls of the bountiful sea veggies. Moana giggled. Turtles could be so silly! For a little while longer, they continued their dive, exploring a nearby rocky reef teeming with sea life.

When it was time for a breath, Moana waved goodbye to Fonu. Then she began her ascent, extending her arms overhead and pulling them back behind her while kicking vigorously. Despite her effort, she didn't travel very far. *That's odd,* she thought. So she tried again, but the result was the same. She must have been caught in the current! *Stay calm,* she reminded herself. *Now is not the time to panic.* Finally she neared the surface, where the sound of thundering waves crashed into her ears. Moana's heart pounded. The signs were undeniable. The stormy seas had arrived. She needed to get to shore, *now.*

Moana resurfaced and gulped in a breath. Treading in place, she looked for the beach—there! It was far away, about a coconut tree's distance from her. As the undertow continued to pull her out to sea, she weighed her options. She could try to escape the current by swimming parallel to the shoreline. Or she could relax and let the water take her out to the deep, where it would release her. Then she could swim around it back to shore.

A large wave made the decision for her. It pummeled her and drove her down, so far down that her ears hurt from the pressure. She paddled her arms and kicked her legs until she burst through the surface of the water once again. Her heart dropped when she saw that she was now the length of two coconut trees away from shore. In the distance, she saw Sina dive into the water. "Mom," Moana yelled, waving both hands back and forth above her head. "Over here!"

But it was too late. A mountainous wave engulfed Moana. Before she knew it, she was deeper underwater than she'd ever been before and losing the energy to swim. As the frigid water squeezed the air out of her lungs, a thick black fog began to fill her vision.

Suddenly she heard a familiar chirp and felt a gentle tug on her wrist. It was Fonu! Moana curled her fingertips around the rim of the turtle's shell and held on as Fonu glided upward. As they broke the surface, Moana drew in a few big breaths. Then Fonu looked back at her. All at once the memory of baby Fonu swimming away safely into the sea all those years ago flooded into Moana's mind. *You remembered,*" she whispered.

The turtle chirped quietly.

"Thank you." Moana strengthened her grip on Fonu's shell and held her breath as the turtle dove back into the ocean. Then Fonu soared under the waves to return Moana to safety—meeting her mother in the shallows.

Before long Moana found herself on the shore in Sina's arms. She hunched over and coughed up water.

Sina gently patted her back. "Are you okay?"

Moana nodded.

Sina cleared her throat. "I'm sorry, Moana. I should have never let you take that last dive. The seas changed so quickly. I thought we had more time."

"So did I," Moana responded. "Now I know better."

They hugged each other tightly.

"If I tell you something," Moana continued, "do you promise to believe me?"

"I will *always* believe you, Moana," Sina said.

"Fonu saved me."

"I know," Sina breathed. "I saw."

Moana felt a warm tear roll down her cheek. Deep down she'd known her mother would believe her, but the proof overwhelmed her with relief.

Sina reached for Moana's hands. "When I was old enough, about your age, my grandmother—your great-grandmother—taught me that our ancestors watched over us through the turtles that called the waters surrounding Motunui their home."

Moana followed Sina's gaze as her mother looked out to the open ocean. Together they watched Fonu lift her head above the water one more time, then disappear into the deep.

Sina turned back to Moana. "My grandmother said, 'We must always protect our ocean guardians, and they will protect us in return.' She made me promise to watch over them. Today, Fonu protected you. Now, Moana, it's your turn. Will you protect Fonu, and all of our ocean guardians, with me?"

"I promise to PROTECT Fonu and ALL of our guardians of the sea,"

Moana repeated proudly.

Sina's eyes twinkled. Then her expression grew grim. "Now, Moana," she said, "you must also promise that you will *never again* go into the water when the signs warn of stormy seas. Nature doesn't give second chances."

"I promise, Mom," Moana replied. She forced a smile, but inside, Sina's warning made her shudder. No, Moana would never forget the power of that ocean. Nor would she ever shake the feeling of almost losing her breath in the cold, deep water. So why would she ever put herself in that danger again?

By the age of sixteen, Moana had assumed many duties in her role as future chief. She believed leadership to be a great privilege, and she spent many of her days caring for her people and their island. But the responsibility came at a cost—diving with Fonu became a rare opportunity. Still, every day, no matter her schedule, she took a trip to the beach to check on her friend.

One morning, outside of her family's *fale*, their open-air home, Moana noticed a billow of low, dark, and thick clouds rolling in from the horizon. She sucked in a sharp breath. These signs were all too familiar.

Sina stepped up behind her.

Moana pointed to the horizon. "Do you see those clouds? They look just like they did *that day*." Her hair stood on end, but she tried her best to shrug off her fear. She was older, stronger, and wiser now, and she had a responsibility as future chief to warn her people about all dangers, including a stormy ocean. She spun around to face her mother. "I'm going to the beach to make sure no one steps a foot into the sea."

"My brave girl," Sina said, reaching for Moana's shoulders. "Just promise me that you will protect yourself as much as you protect everyone else."

Moana nodded firmly.

"Okay, then," Sina replied. "I'll be right here if you need me."

Moana kissed her mother and raced to the beach.

There, the waves thundered and crashed, creating a deafening sound rivaled only by the wind that howled and screeched. The seas were already very stormy, just as Moana had predicted. She shielded her eyes from the sand that whipped into her face as she surveyed the ocean for swimmers.

On one end of the beach, two fishermen emerged from the pounding shore break. Moana dashed over to them as they pulled themselves up onto the sand. "Are you all right?"

"We're okay," one fisherman heaved, "but we lost *everything* . . . our best net . . . two of our traps. The waves, they were like *mountains*. They came out of nowhere."

"Did you see anyone else out there?" Moana asked.

"No, just us," he replied.

Moana let out a quiet sigh of relief.

"We'll have to wait out the weather before coming back to salvage our net and traps."

Moana watched the fishermen trudge away, then turned her attention back to the ocean. Its choppy white crests crashed together, forming a fog of sea spray that burned Moana's eyes. *A person would have to be really gutsy to swim in the ocean at a time like this,* she mused to herself.

Moana was turning to leave the beach when, just at that moment, an unusual sight caught her eye. On the surface of the water, a little brown spot floated. It looked like something was caught in a fishing net. She squinted her eyes to get a better look. Then a tangled turtle came into focus. "FONU!" she cried.

Moana dashed to the waterline. Her heart drummed in her chest. She had promised Sina she wouldn't ever go out into a stormy sea. She had almost drowned last time, after all. But she had also vowed to protect Fonu.

Into the water she dove! Down, down, down she swam, under the waves. They shook her ferociously to and fro, and she struggled to hold her breath, but not even the raging sea could stop her from helping her friend.

Moana resurfaced next to Fonu. The turtle chirped and tried to paddle her flippers, but the net bound them in place. Fonu was in trouble! As Moana fumbled with the slippery rope, a set of waves roared toward them.

Thinking quickly, Moana balled up the net and wedged it in between her and Fonu. Then she grabbed the sides of Fonu's shell and turned toward the shore. "We're going under!" she exclaimed. She heard the turtle blow out air. Then Moana duck dove down, under the waves, holding Fonu in front of her and the net in between them, kicking with all her might. Her lungs burned like they were on fire, and her aching legs passed the point of exhaustion, but she kept kicking.

At last, they arrived on the shore. The same turtle that glided weightlessly through the water was so heavy on land. Moana drove her legs into the sand and cried out in agony as she pushed Fonu out of the water's reach.

Fonu chirped weakly.

"Don't worry, Fonu," Moana panted. "I'll help you."

She took hold of the net and ran her fingers along the rope until she found where it was knotted. Her people were master netmakers, and this knot was very complicated. She'd need something sharp to cut it—and a little extra help.

"I'll be right back," she called to Fonu as she ran toward the village.

A few moments later, Moana burst into her family's fale. To her surprise, she saw no sign of Sina.

"Up here," Sina called, then jumped down from a post. She wiped sweat from her brow and looked up. "This wind is really doing a number on our roof." Sina glanced at Moana, then leveled her gaze. "*Why* are you soaking wet?"

"Mom, don't get upset . . . but I-I need your help. *We* need your help."

"Who's *we*?"

"Me and Fonu. She's trapped in a net. We need something to cut it. I had to swim out—"

"You *what*?" Sina threw her hands in the air. "Moana, what is wrong with you?"

Moana gulped down tears. "*I* made a promise to Fonu that I would protect her. *You* made a promise to my great-grandmother that you would protect turtles like her, too. I'm sorry, Mom, that I've upset you. But Fonu needs our help *right now*. And I *can't* do it alone. Will you help me?"

Sina paused. Then she grabbed her sharp stone adze. "This will slice through anything. Let's go."

Back on the sand, Moana found Fonu twisted tighter in the twine. Her stomach sickened when she noticed that one of the turtle's flippers was extended in an unnatural way.

"She's trying to get back into the water," Moana said urgently. "We need to move quickly!"

Sina's eyes flashed. She dropped to her knees and grabbed the rope. Moana held on to the other end where it was knotted. Sina rubbed the rock adze back and forth under the knot until the rope split apart. Then she wove the ends over, under, around, and through to untangle the trapped turtle. Once freed, Fonu flapped her flippers.

Moana pumped her fists into the air. "Mom, you did it!" she hollered. "Now let's get her back into the water."

They each grabbed one side of Fonu's shell. Like guiding a canoe into the sea, they carefully pushed her, headfirst, across the sand until she floated on the water. But the poor turtle was too exhausted to swim through the treacherous shore break. When a wave crashed on her, she tumbled back onto the sand.

They tried again.

"Now!" Moana yelled, in between the rows of rumbling

whitewater. This time they pushed Fonu *hard*. The turtle skimmed across the water's surface from the force. As a wave approached her, she paddled her flippers . . . and crested over it!

As Fonu disappeared behind the wave, Moana cupped her hands around her mouth and let out a big cheer. *"Woo-hoo!"*

But then the water leveled, exposing a behemoth wave barreling toward Fonu. "Oh, no," Sina cried as the wave sucked up the turtle and spat her back onto the sand.

A pain shot through Moana's chest. Her palms got sweaty and her knees felt weak. *Stay calm,* she thought. *Now is not the time to panic.* She closed her eyes and listened to the tempestuous ocean, asking for a sign.

Suddenly, a quiet filled her ears. It was a cold quiet, the sound of the deep. The place, Moana realized, where Fonu needed to be. *Under* the waves. She opened her eyes and gazed resolutely into the sea.

Just then, as if Sina had read her mind, Moana felt her mother's fingers interlace with hers. "I trust you," Sina said.

Moana turned to her mother and squeezed her hand. "Follow my lead."

Back to Fonu they both ran. There, once again, they each grabbed a side of Fonu's shell and slid her into the water. But this time . . . "One, two, three!" Moana shouted as they dove in with the turtle.

Down, down, down they swam, holding Fonu in front of them as they kicked with all their might, following the ocean floor. The current pushed them in every direction, but they kept swimming.

Soon they arrived at the drop-off point, where the seafloor fell away and the deep ocean began. Sina led Moana's hand to the side

of Fonu's shell that she held and wrapped Moana's fingers around it. Moana nodded at Sina. Then Sina lowered her legs, planted her feet into the sand, and gave Moana a great push.

The push propelled Moana into the cold, quiet waters where Fonu had saved her life years before. The place where Moana knew Fonu would be safe. All at once, the turtle began to paddle her flippers. And with a mighty *flap*, Fonu descended into the deep.

Joy rippled through Moana. But the celebration would have to wait—she still had to swim back to shore!

She took a big stroke and thought of Fonu, her beloved friend who had protected her all these years. She stroked again, thinking of her mother, who trusted her and helped her protect her friend. And with another stroke, she thought of her ancestors, who, like her, protected the great turtles of the deep and were protected by them in return.

In the shallows, Sina wrapped her arms around Moana and lifted her out of the water. They hobbled to shore and collapsed on the sand under the safety of a pandanus tree. For a moment they sat in silence, taking in the experience they had just shared.

Then Sina turned to Moana. "My brave, brave girl," she said, cupping Moana's face. "You saved Fonu. And you honored our family's duty to protect our ocean guardians."

Moana placed her hands over her mother's. "No, Mom," she said. "*We* did. We did it *together*. Great-Grandmother would be so proud of us."

Sina's eyes sparkled. "You're right, my little minnow. She would be. I know I am."

Moana leaned in and pressed her nose and forehead against her mother's. Sina pressed back. "I love you, Mom," said Moana as they released their *hongi*.

"And I love you, too, Moana," Sina replied.

Just then, rain began pouring from the skies.

"We should *probably* head home," Sina said with a laugh, holding out her hand to Moana, who lifted herself up against it.

"You know, Mom"—Moana winked—"our people say that rain is a blessing."

"I know," Sina said, playfully nudging Moana with her hip. "I taught you that. But you wanna know something else?"

"What?" asked Moana, offering her arm to her mother.

Sina took Moana's arm. "You're *my* blessing," she said with a squeeze.

Together they walked home, drenched from the rain, grateful for each other and for the guardians of the sea.

How do you show GRATITUDE to your FRIENDS?

MULAN

Mulan has always struggled to fit in. She wants to bring her family honor, but isn't sure how to do so while remaining true to herself. When her father is called to serve in the Imperial army, Mulan seizes the opportunity to do right by her family. Disguising herself as a man, Mulan joins the army in her father's place and shows incredible bravery in fighting the Huns. Through courage, passion, and determination, she proves that anything is possible when you believe in yourself.

THE VILLAGE HERO

WRITTEN BY MARIE CHOW & ILLUSTRATED BY ALICE X. ZHANG AND STUDIO IBOIX

SPECIAL THANKS TO CULTURAL CONSULTANTS DAVID LIN, FLORA ZHAO, AND BILL IMADA AT IW GROUP

"**M**ulan! Always the early riser!" said Lingling with a broad grin.

Mulan waved to the stable boy and dismounted from Khan. She had just come back from a ride in the woods, where she could be alone with her thoughts.

"You know me," she replied with a modest shrug. She tried to smooth her hair into some sort of order, embarrassed to find at least two leaves and a small twig tangled in it.

As she led her horse to its stall and closed the gate, Tsai'er, the village scholar, approached. "Had a good ride?" he asked.

Mulan nodded politely and then stifled a sigh. She wasn't used to all the attention that came with being a war hero. Young men wanted to train with her or marry her; young women wanted to befriend her or be like her. It was unsettling.

As she made her way toward home, more neighbors greeted her with compliments and questions. It took several minutes of nodding and *mmm-hmm*ing politely before Mulan finally escaped the well-wishers.

She turned the corner onto a quiet street and almost ran into her neighbor Mei, who was struggling to carry three lanterns and a woven bag. Mei managed to juggle the lanterns without dropping one, but she lost her grip on the bag.

MULAN IS . . .

STRONG-WILLED
COURAGEOUS
RESOURCEFUL
FEARLESS
A TEAM PLAYER
THOUGHTFUL

MULAN'S DREAM:

To bring honor to her family

HEROIC MOMENT:

Saving the Emperor from
the Huns

SIDEKICK:

Mushu

FAMOUS QUOTE:

"My name is Mulan. I did it to
save my father. . . . It was the
only way."

Mulan dove for it, nearly
tripping over her own feet before
she righted herself with the bag
dangling gracelessly from one
arm. "Ta-da?" she said sheepishly.

Mei chuckled. "Thank you,"
she said, grimacing as she tried to
take the bag back.

Mulan waved Mei's hand away.
"If you're going home, I might as
well carry it for you. I'm headed
that way, too."

"I'd appreciate it," the older girl
said, shifting the three lanterns in
her arms. "These aren't heavy, or
even that big, but they are—"

"Awkward?" Mulan laughed,
happy to be having a normal
conversation for once. It
seemed that everyone else she
encountered went out of their way
to compliment her health, Khan's
grooming, or the honor she
brought to her family.

Mulan eyed the lanterns Mei
carried. "Did you make all three
of those lanterns for this week's

festival?" she asked. "I'm still not done with mine—and I'm only decorating one!"

Mei chuckled. "I can't help myself. I know that most families make one lantern with a simpler design, but I've always been *san xin er yi*—three hearts, one mind. I can never settle on just one idea."

Mei had always looked forward to the Lantern Festival. In villages and cities all over China, people gathered at local temples to display their handmade lanterns and place candles inside to usher in the coming spring. Mei's favorite part of the tradition was making the lanterns. Year after year, her designs had become more complex and beautiful with practice.

The girls stopped walking as Mei held out the lanterns and Mulan examined each in turn. Like the lanterns other villagers made, Mei's were made of silk wrapped around a wood frame, and two handspans in height, but the similarities ended there.

"You've been so clever about these designs," Mulan said, admiring the Chinese symbols and tree shapes that Mei had embroidered on each one. "They're wonderful alone, but when combined, the characters make the word 'forest'!"

Mei bowed her head. "I've always liked playing around with words."

Mulan handed the lanterns back as the girls continued walking. "When we light them, I'm sure everyone will appreciate what you've done." Her face brightened as she continued. "I love when we're all gathered and enjoying the glow from the lanterns together. It's one of my favorite traditions."

Mei turned toward Mulan in surprise. "I never would've guessed you cared so much about tradition."

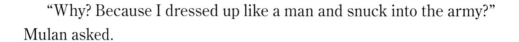

"Why? Because I dressed up like a man and snuck into the army?" Mulan asked.

> **"A girl can't BREAK THE RULES and still like TRADITION?"**

Mulan's tone was playful, so Mei laughed in response. But her face flushed. "I'm sorry, was that rude? All I meant to say was, it's certainly not what most girls would have done."

Mulan shook her head. "I'm not offended. Actually, it's nice *not* to be complimented for once."

Mei gave Mulan a questioning look.

"It sounds ungrateful to complain about compliments, and I know everyone means well," Mulan started, looking down at her feet. "But I'm still the same girl I was before the war. I still can't sew or cook. I can't embroider lanterns or remember the eight virtues that the Matchmaker wanted me to learn. When I joined the army, I wanted to bring honor to my family, not . . ."

"Endless attention to yourself?" Mei asked, finishing Mulan's sentence for her.

Mulan looked up at her neighbor. "I take it you've noticed?"

As the two girls shared a quiet moment of understanding, Mulan found herself wondering why the two of them had never spoken before. Mei was only a couple of years older than Mulan, and they'd been neighbors for years. Mulan supposed she'd always just assumed they had nothing in common. After all, Mulan didn't have a lot in common with most girls.

As they arrived at Mei's home, a few of the younger neighbor girls came up to Mulan, hoping for a moment with the village star. Mei took the bag Mulan had been carrying for her, and, with a parting smile to her new friend, went quietly into her home.

At home, Mei opened her bag and examined the silk fibers she'd purchased in the market. Quilting was something her mother had taught her, and Mei took pride in every part of the process. There was something calming about combining fibers to make thread, layering the cloth, sewing the pieces together, and embroidering the intricate designs, knowing that each part had been made with love and that each creation was unique.

Mei felt the same about making the lanterns: creating beautiful works of art was her way of bringing honor to her family.

Her father came out of his bedroom. "I saw you talking to Mulan outside," he said, sitting down across the table from Mei. "What a daughter she has turned out to be. She has brought great honor to the Fa family."

"Yes. And she's still humble," Mei replied. "A little different from other girls in our village."

"You'd do well to learn from her," her father said. "That's what the matchmakers want these days. A girl like Mulan."

Mei bowed her head. "Yes, Baba. I understand."

"That girl can do anything," he continued. "I hear she rides a horse better than any man in our village."

Like the rest of the villagers, Mei admired Mulan for what the girl had done. She couldn't imagine disguising herself as a soldier, summoning the courage to join the army, training among warriors, or wielding any weapon heavier than a kitchen knife. She wouldn't have known how to fight one enemy, much less win an entire war. Perhaps more important, Mei wasn't sure she would have been brave enough to do any of these things if they'd been asked of her.

Mei blinked and focused on the quilt she was making. She told herself it didn't matter whether other people noticed the care she put into her art. It was enough for Mei to know it was a job well done. While Mei could not control how similar she was, or wasn't, to Mulan, she knew she had her own strengths: she could make beautiful things with her hands. She wished her father could be proud of her, and the skills she did possess. But she also wished she could be brave, like Mulan, the village hero.

A week later, the night of the Lantern Festival had finally arrived. The whole village was abuzz about the night's festivities, when everyone would walk up the hill to the newly constructed temple and place candles in their lanterns, sing songs, and tell riddles.

Mulan and Mei both left their homes just as the sun was setting, and they began walking along the path together. Mulan looked at the lantern Mei was carrying. "You didn't bring all three!"

Mei shrugged. "I never intended to bring all of them. I just like to have a backup and, you know, a backup for the backup."

"Well, which one did you pick?" Mulan asked.

Mei turned her lantern around so Mulan could see the design.

Mulan moved to the side of the road and put her own lantern down before taking Mei's creation, holding it up to the waning sunlight. "I love how you've embroidered the leaves," Mulan said. "Once you put the candle inside, the light will filter through in such a beautiful pattern!"

Mei tilted her head, shyly accepting her lantern back from Mulan. "You've looked at it more closely than even my father."

"I'm fairly certain *my* father's just happy I finished mine in time. He always says I should know my strengths . . . and be honest about my weaknesses. Embroidering, sewing, cooking—none of these are particular talents of mine."

Mei sighed. "Consider yourself lucky," she said under her breath.

"What do you mean?" Mulan asked.

Mei blushed, almost wishing she hadn't said anything. But she couldn't shake the unspoken disappointment of her father's gaze, one that seemed to have eyes only for Mulan's accomplishments. "I suppose I meant that cooking and sewing won't bring honor to my family. Just ask my father."

Mulan gave a snort. "What's that old saying? That dynasties are easier to change than personalities? People still value the same things they did yesterday. I look forward to the day when I can go back to being plain old Mulan, when the only thing anyone would say to me was that my rice pudding was tasteless."

Mei laughed. "Rice pudding's a specialty of mine, actually. I could teach you if—"

"Mulan!" Tsai'er the scholar shouted from across the road,

dragging his grown son in his wake. "My son Daqing wanted to say hello to the village's great hero."

Daqing, who had always been shy, looked down at the ground and then at his father, a bit helplessly. "Hello, Mulan," he said, his face burning red. After a pause, he raised his eyes and said as an afterthought, "Hello, Mei."

Tsai'er nudged his son and mumbled, "What a lovely lantern you've made, Mulan."

Daqing parroted, "What a lovely lantern you've made, Mulan." He reached for Mei's lantern, which Mulan was still holding.

"Actually, this beautiful creation is Mei's," Mulan replied.

Daqing dropped the lantern in his embarrassment. Mulan and Mei both reached for it, but bumped into each other in the process. Tsai'er stepped backward to avoid having the girls crash into him— and accidentally kicked Mei's lantern, which rolled down the hill before anyone could grab it.

Mei watched helplessly as Mulan chased after the lantern. She knew the lantern was ruined before Mulan picked it up, exposing gaping tears in the silk.

The group went silent. Tears slowly filled Mei's eyes.

Daqing spoke first. "I am so very sorry. I didn't mean—"

"It's okay," Mei said, her voice steady.

For a moment, everyone's gaze was on Mulan as she carried the ruined lantern up the hill. She ran her hand softly over the embroidered tree, which had started to unravel.

"It's really okay," Mei said again. She opened her mouth to say something else, but her breath caught in her throat. Her gaze locked on something in the distance behind the group.

Without another word, Mei started to run back toward the village.

Daqing frowned and peered sheepishly at Mulan. "I tried to apologize," he said.

"I know it was an accident," Mulan said, watching Mei's retreating back. That's when she finally noticed what had caught Mei's eye: a plume of smoke, unmistakable in its color and intensity. This was no cooking fire—it was too dark and ashy for that. Without another word, Mulan took off after Mei.

As she ran, Mulan couldn't quite pinpoint where the fire was, only that it was near the back of the village. The horse stalls? She hoped not. The hay would make the fire impossible to control, and Khan and the other horses would be trapped. The old temple? A definite possibility. Mulan had overheard some of the villagers say they still planned on hanging a lantern there, even though the new temple had finally been completed.

As she came closer, she saw it was indeed the old temple that had caught fire. Mulan covered her mouth and nose with her sleeve and ran into the burning building. Inside the temple, her eyes watered within seconds from the sting of smoke. Flames licked up the temple's wall next to the blackened shell of a lantern, which Mulan guessed was the source of the fire.

Where would she find enough water to put out the flames? Her home was only down the road, but Mulan knew that her family had already used most of the water she'd carried from the well that morning. The well itself was much farther away, almost in the center of the village, and the river, in the opposite direction, would take even longer to reach.

As Mulan weighed the various options, she also took a moment to

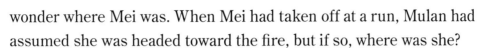

wonder where Mei was. When Mei had taken off at a run, Mulan had assumed she was headed toward the fire, but if so, where was she?

Mulan began backing out of the temple. Heading into the village would at least increase the odds of running into someone else, of being able to organize help. She nearly crashed into Mei, who was just heading in, struggling to carry a vase of water and a pile of quilts.

"Take this," Mei said, putting down the vase and handing Mulan a quilt. "I brought water, too, but I couldn't carry enough to make a difference. I'm hoping these quilts will help."

As Mulan unfurled the quilt in her hands, she couldn't help noticing its intricate embroidery and beautiful design. There was no doubt in Mulan's mind that this was Mei's handiwork.

Mei unfolded her quilt and started fanning the flames, coughing as the smoke filled the room. Mulan followed suit, whipping the beautiful blanket at the fire. But soon the girls realized that their efforts were only spreading the flames.

"What do we do now?" Mulan asked Mei.

The girls looked around themselves and at each other, an idea sparking in their minds at the same time.

Mei started, "What if we use the water—"

"—to dampen the quilts?" Mulan finished.

For a brief moment, the girls shared a smile, sensing a spark of true friendship between them.

"Are you ready?" Mulan asked.

"Let's do this," Mei said. A surge of adrenaline zipped up her spine.

Mei poured the water from the vase she had brought onto both blankets. The two girls worked together to smother the flames with the dampened quilts, which had become heavy with absorbed water.

Little by little, they put out the worst of the blaze, but there were still smaller fires and embers glowing all around them, any one of which could burst into an inferno at any moment.

Mulan continued to fight the flames, her eyes streaming with tears from the smoke. Mei began coughing harder, and Mulan turned around just in time to see the girl collapse.

Mulan ran to Mei's side and quickly wrapped a singed quilt around her. Then she scooped Mei into her arms, thankful for all the strength training she'd gotten in the army, and carried her outside the temple to safety.

By then, a large crowd had gathered. Several villagers ran inside the temple carrying small tankards of water to put out the remaining flames. The others swarmed around the girls, stepping back only when Mulan urged them to give Mei enough space and air to recover.

The villagers spoke over one another in their excitement:

"You put the fire out so quickly!"

"How did you do it?"

"Mulan, are you hurt?"

"Of course she's not hurt. Mulan saved the day again. The girl's invincible!"

As the villagers babbled, Mulan focused on Mei, propping her up so she could breathe. At last, Mei coughed and slowly opened her eyes.

The villagers quieted down as Mulan explained what had happened. "It was Mei who noticed the fire first, and who was level-headed enough to bring these quilts from her home." She paused, running her fingertips over Mei's beautiful embroidery, which was now singed and ruined. "She deserves the credit for controlling the blaze."

Mei shook her head. "I couldn't have done it alone. You were so brave, and I just—" She started coughing again.

Mulan's face turned serious. "You showed true courage today, Mei."

"Well, I learned from the best," said Mei, blushing.

As Mulan helped Mei to her feet, Tsai'er clapped his hands together. "What a fortunate village we are! To have two female heroes!"

"Mei's the hero today," Mulan said firmly.

Mei's father nodded. "I agree," he said, smiling in approval. He looked at his daughter. "You have made your family very proud."

And with that, everyone cheered.

Mei's eyes watered—either from the smoke or her father's words.

Daqing handed Mulan and Mei cups of water as an unspoken apology for earlier. "Did you make this quilt?" he asked Mei, who nodded.

"Then perhaps you would sew one for our family," Tsai'er suggested. "It would be an honor to display such a beautiful quilt made by the young woman who saved the old temple."

The other villagers nodded and started putting in their own requests for Mei's handiwork as her father looked on proudly.

Mulan laughed. "Looks like I'll have to learn about lanterns *and* sewing from you. I wish you'd been with me in the army. I could've used your creative problem-solving when I was trying *not* to burn down the palace!"

Mei gave a sly smile. "I'll teach you how to quilt—if you teach me how to ride a horse!"

"It's a deal," Mulan agreed. "I think we'll make a great team."

What was
YOUR
BRAVEST
moment?

CINDERELLA

Cinderella is warm and sincere with everyone she meets. Whether it's the smallest mouse or the King himself, she treats everyone with equal respect. In spite of the harsh treatment she receives from her stepfamily, Cinderella remains a kind, loving girl. While she makes the best of her situation, she continues to dream of a better life and believes there is good in everyone.

A SWEET SALON

WRITTEN BY AUBRE ANDRUS & ILLUSTRATED BY ALINA CHAU

Sweep the floors. Polish the silverware. Fluff the pillows. Hem the dresses. Cinderella's morning was filled with chores, as usual. But she couldn't stop smiling as she worked. Her stepmother, Lady Tremaine, was hosting a salon at their home that afternoon. A salon was a special monthly event where Lady Tremaine invited the most gifted women in the kingdom to the château to share their talents. Cinderella loved humming along to their beautiful musical performances, gasping at their dramatic readings, and swooning over singsong poetry. Cinderella didn't even mind serving tea and finger sandwiches while she got to watch such fascinating performances.

Cinderella had been so inspired by these talented women that she had written and memorized a poem of her own. She dreamed of one day performing it aloud—hopefully at that day's salon. All morning she'd been mustering up enough courage to ask her stepmother. She was just waiting for the right opportunity.

As she swept the hallway floor, Cinderella began practicing her poem. "Starlight, moonlight—"

"This calls for a duel!" Drizella yelled from the music room down the hall. Drizella and Anastasia were Cinderella's stepsisters. They were practicing a scene from a play they would be performing at the salon. Drizella's voice sounded hoarse from reciting her lines so many times.

CINDERELLA IS . . .

OPTIMISTIC
CONSCIENTIOUS
WITTY
GRACEFUL
A DREAMER
ATTENTIVE

CINDERELLA'S DREAM:

To build a better life

HEROIC MOMENT:

Standing up for herself to fight for a better future

SIDEKICKS:

Jaq and Gus

FAMOUS QUOTE:

"A dream is a wish your heart makes."

"Not on my watch," Anastasia shouted.

"Stop! I need more emotion, Anastasia," Lady Tremaine demanded. "How am I to believe this scene if I can't sense what your character is feeling? Do it again!"

"I can't do this many more times, Mother," Drizella complained. "My throat hurts!"

Lady Tremaine rolled her eyes. "From the top, girls."

Drizella cleared her throat. "This calls for—" She stopped and wrapped a hand around her neck. "My throat!" was all she managed to say before breaking into a coughing fit.

"I said from the top, Drizella!" Lady Tremaine demanded.

"This calls for—" Drizella tried before having another cough attack.

Lady Tremaine threw her hands in the air. "All the ladies will be watching your performance and judging you. Judging *all* of us!" she said to her daughters. "Go to your rooms and rest up. I'm expecting an excellent performance from you this afternoon!"

Drizella and Anastasia started marching out of the music room just as Cinderella walked past them dreamily. The stepsisters shared a suspicious look. What was Cinderella smiling about? They stepped into the hallway and eavesdropped as Cinderella approached Lady Tremaine.

"Stepmother? I wrote a poem I'd like to perform at the salon today," Cinderella said.

"Is that so?" Lady Tremaine asked.

"I've been practicing very hard, and—"

"Let's hear it," Lady Tremaine said.

"Starlight, moonlight . . ." Cinderella recited the poem perfectly for her stepmother. Her voice was clear and strong. She didn't forget a single word. And the poem was beautiful.

Anastasia and Drizella huffed in disbelief. They'd had no idea Cinderella was so good at reciting poetry—and they didn't like it.

Lady Tremaine looked down her nose at Cinderella. "*If* all of your chores are done, *if* the tea service is complete, and *if* there is time at the end, I *might* allow you to read one poem."

Cinderella was shocked—and her stepsisters even more so. Before Cinderella could see them, Anastasia and Drizella stormed down the hallway toward their bedrooms, stunned that their mother was letting Cinderella get some attention at the day's salon.

"Oh, thank you, Stepmother," Cinderella said, trying to mask her excitement.

"And make sure you look presentable today," Lady Tremaine

added. "No dirty work clothes. Change into your formal serving dress and fix your hair nicely."

"Of course, Stepmother." Cinderella beamed. "I won't let you down."

Cinderella walked down the hallway with an even bigger smile. She was hopeful that her dream would come true this afternoon. But first she had to finish up her chores. And take care of Drizella's sore throat. Cinderella ran to the kitchen to fetch a cup of hot water with lemon. That always made Cinderella's throat feel better. Her stepsisters weren't always friendly, but she knew how important this performance was to both Anastasia and Drizella. With any luck, Drizella's throat would heal quickly with some rest and a warm drink.

Drizella was pouting, lying under the covers. Anastasia stood, staring at herself in the mirror. She was brushing her hair over and over again while practicing her lines.

Cinderella rapped on the door before she stepped inside.

"What do you want?" Anastasia asked.

"Here," Cinderella said as she walked toward Drizella. "This might help."

Drizella grabbed the teacup from Cinderella's hands, then sipped the hot water and lemon slowly.

"I hope you feel—" Cinderella began to say.

"You can leave now," Anastasia said as she pushed Cinderella out the door. "We need to rest our voices for this afternoon's performance. I can't do my scene without Drizella!"

"Can you believe her?" Anastasia said to Drizella as she shut the door. Drizella was too busy drinking from her teacup to answer. "And

she thinks she can perform a poem at the salon today when *we* might not even be able to do *our* scene. It's not fair!"

Drizella opened her mouth to interject. What she wanted to say was, "Of course we'll be able to do our scene!" But what came out was . . . nothing. She grabbed her throat. She opened her mouth again and whispered, "My voice!" And then she started coughing again.

"Drizella, speak up!" Anastasia was panic-stricken. "Talk louder!"

Drizella shook her head as she continued to cough.

"I can't do my scene without you! I'll look ridiculous!" Anastasia paced the room. "We must perform today. Everyone is expecting it! We're the ladies of this house!"

Drizella held up the teacup with a grimace on her face. She pretended to be serving the tea and then pointed toward the door Cinderella had just stepped through.

Anastasia gasped as she realized what Drizella was trying to tell her. "Do you think? *Cinderella?!* What did she put in that tea?!" She stormed toward the door, prepared to charge after Cinderella. But then she stopped.

"Wait," Anastasia said. "She's just jealous of us. She wants to make sure she has time for her stupid little poem. If she tried to ruin our performance, then we're just going to have to ruin hers."

Drizella smiled wickedly in agreement.

Cinderella's sweet mouse pals Perla and Jaq were taking a post-lunch nap after an adventurous encounter with Lucifer, Lady Tremaine's mischievous cat. They had successfully gathered enough corn kernels to feed all the other mice that lived at the château, but now they were exhausted. They sank cozily into a basket of soft fabric scraps in the corner of Cinderella's room. When Cinderella returned after finishing her chores, they'd tell her all about it.

The door creaked. Jaq opened one eye. But it wasn't Cinderella.

"There it is!" Anastasia whispered. She was panting after climbing up the long staircase that led to Cinderella's bedroom.

She and Drizella elbowed each other as they entered, the hoops of their fancy dresses barely squeezing through the door. Anastasia quickly grabbed a dress that was hanging from a changing screen: the outfit that Cinderella had set out to wear to the salon. Drizella snatched two other dresses that were folded in a basket right next to Jaq and Perla.

Perla woke Jaq, whose eyes shot open. Perla swiftly covered her friend's mouth so he wouldn't say anything. Jaq quickly realized what was going on. He saw Drizella grab Cinderella's only clean apron, too.

"Her clothes! Her clothes!" Jaq managed to squeak out despite Perla's best efforts. Luckily, Anastasia and Drizella had already turned their backs and were heading out the door. As they elbowed their way back out, a purple feather fell out of Drizella's hair.

"What are they doing? Where did they go?" Jaq asked Perla. "They stole Cinderelly's nice things!"

"What do we do?" Perla asked.

"I wait. I tell Cinderelly as soon as she get here," Jaq said. "You go. You follow them."

"Okay!" Perla ran through a crack in the wall while Jaq retrieved Drizella's feather. He sat and stared at the door, wishing Cinderella would hurry. Where was she? It was getting late!

A little while later, Cinderella ran through the door, quickly closing it behind her while removing her dirty apron.

"I'm running behind!" Cinderella said aloud to herself. "Now where is my—"

"Cinderelly! Cinderelly!" Jaq jumped up and down and waved the feather. "They stole your dress! They took all of your clothes!"

"Who?" Cinderella ducked down and picked up Jaq. She studied the purple feather.

"Anastasia! Drizelly!"

"Now why would they . . ." Cinderella trailed off and set Jaq gently on her vanity before taking a seat. She looked in the mirror. Her dress was dirty. Her hair was frizzled. And she could hear carriages pulling up to the château. The guests were already arriving. Lady Tremaine would not allow Cinderella to serve her guests in dirty work clothes. How could she look presentable without the dress that Anastasia and Drizella had just stolen? Not only would she let Lady Tremaine down, but if Cinderella couldn't attend the salon, then she definitely couldn't perform her poem.

"Oh, Jaq," Cinderella said. "I was really looking forward to the salon. This was my chance to speak up and have my voice heard. The message in this poem is important to me."

Jaq felt sad for Cinderella. She had worked so hard cleaning. She had worked so hard writing and memorizing her poem. She always worked so hard—and never got rewarded. Before he could say anything, he heard footsteps charging up the spiral staircase that led to Cinderella's room. The door burst open.

"Get up, child! Why are you not dressed?" Lady Tremaine hissed. Anastasia and Drizella fluttered behind her, eager to watch Cinderella get into trouble.

"My formal serving dress is missing, Stepmother," Cinderella said as she stood.

"How could you misplace one of the few dresses you own?" Lady Tremaine looked around the room as Anastasia snickered.

Cinderella wiped at a smudge on her skirt. "If you just give me some extra time, I'm happy to clean up the dress I'm wearing—"

"Not a chance!" Anastasia scoffed.

Lady Tremaine sneered and turned to her daughters. "You two need to greet the guests while I deal with this," she told them. "Repeat after me: Welcome to our château. It's lovely to see you."

"Welcome to our château," Anastasia repeated. But when Drizella opened her mouth, only the faintest whisper came out.

"Drizella, speak up!" Lady Tremaine said.

Drizella opened her mouth. Nothing came out.

"You've lost your voice?!" Lady Tremaine threw her hands up in the air. "Why didn't you tell me?" She glared at Anastasia.

"Mother, I . . ." Anastasia started.

But Lady Tremaine wasn't listening. She paced the room, looking from Cinderella to Drizella and back again. "Drizella, out of your dress. Give it to Cinderella. And Cinderella, give your work dress to Drizella."

Drizella's mouth dropped open.

"But, Mother!" Anastasia yelled. "You can't expect Drizella to attend the salon wearing that old thing!"

"Without a voice, Drizella *isn't* going to the salon at all. Drizella, you need rest. Head straight to your room once you've changed. Anastasia, you'll perform both parts in your play now."

Anastasia and Drizella looked at each other with wide eyes. Their plan had backfired. Stealing Cinderella's clothes had not helped them at all. In fact, it had made things worse. Much worse. Anastasia couldn't perform both parts. She could barely perform her own lines. And now Drizella wouldn't even be able to attend! Meanwhile, Cinderella got to wear a beautiful dress and go to the salon. And possibly even perform her poem!

"But, Mother, I can't do both roles!" Anastasia cried.

"You don't have a choice. I expect you and Cinderella in the salon in five minutes," Lady Tremaine said, starting toward the door. "And, Anastasia, fix your hair."

Anastasia reached for her head and felt that her feather was missing.

"Looking for this?" Cinderella said, handing over the purple feather. "It ended up in my room somehow."

Anastasia's eyes grew wide as she grabbed the feather. Then she quickly turned around and followed her mother down the stairs.

Drizella sneered as she changed out of her dress and handed it to Cinderella. "The next time you and Anastasia want to borrow my dresses, just ask," Cinderella said to Drizella. Of course, she knew that her stepsisters hadn't really borrowed the dresses—they had stolen them to hurt her. "But I do expect them to be returned to me after the salon."

Drizella couldn't say anything, so she slipped into Cinderella's work dress and disappeared down the stairs in a huff.

Cinderella looked at herself in the mirror. She had always admired Drizella's green gown, but never dreamed she'd have a chance to wear it. But she couldn't dwell on that. She quickly brushed her hair and pinned it up. She needed to get downstairs to prepare the tea for the guests. She would only be able to perform her poem at the salon if it started on time.

"Good luck, Cinderelly!" Jaq said. "Perla and I will find your missing clothes. I'll go help her now!"

"Thank you, Jaq! You're a good friend," Cinderella said as she shut the door and hurried down the steps.

The ladies of the kingdom had already taken seats in the padded chairs and couches arranged around the music room. Cinderella carefully delivered tea while the guests took turns performing. One woman played a happy melody on the flute. As Cinderella served the finger sandwiches, another guest read an excerpt from an adventure story that made Cinderella's heart flutter. The next woman sang a sweet lullaby while Cinderella cleaned up the plates. While she refilled tea, she overheard fascinating conversations about literature and new inventions from faraway places. There was so much for her to learn! Finally, as she began serving cake and cookies, Lady Tremaine stepped to the front of the room.

"Thank you all for attending. It's getting late. The last performance of the day will be my daughter, Anastasia."

Cinderella watched with a heavy heart as Anastasia scurried to the front of the room. Lady Tremaine's promise had been that Cinderella could perform *if and only if* there was time. And there wasn't enough time after all. Today was not the day that she would be able to recite her poem. At least she'd gotten to attend the salon. But it was a small consolation considering all the effort she had put in.

Anastasia looked around. "T-today, I will be . . . um, performing a scene," she stammered nervously. She fidgeted with her dress as she tried to remember Drizella's first line. She took a deep breath.

"This calls for a duel!" she shouted, with her right arm pointed toward where Drizella should have been standing. Then she jumped to her right and stuck up her left arm.

"Not on my watch," she yelled a little too loudly. Someone in the front row started giggling, and a few others joined in. Anastasia jumped to her left and stuck up her right arm again.

"I said stand back!" Now the audience's giggles had turned into loud belly laughs. Anastasia turned bright red. She couldn't believe everyone thought her dramatic play was funny!

Lady Tremaine backed into the corner of the room, unsure how to gracefully stop the play without embarrassing her daughter even more.

Cinderella watched as Anastasia stumbled through a few more lines and jumped from side to side. She had listened to her stepsisters rehearse this play repeatedly over the past few weeks. She had it memorized. She set her tray down on a table and charged toward the front of the room.

"I will never stand down!" Cinderella projected Drizella's line toward the audience, then turned toward Anastasia.

"I will always STAND UP for what I BELIEVE IN. No matter what it takes."

The laughing stopped. All the women of the kingdom were enchanted by Cinderella's performance. Anastasia looked stunned, but continued with her lines. As the scene continued, Cinderella tried not to make eye contact with Lady Tremaine. She didn't know whether her stepmother would be relieved—or furious.

When Cinderella and Anastasia took a bow, the audience clapped and cheered.

"Encore! Encore!" they cried.

Lady Tremaine quieted the audience.

"I'm so pleased that you enjoyed the performance by my lovely daughter Anastasia and my stepdaughter, Cinderella," Lady Tremaine said. "If you insist, Cinderella has one more performance for us today."

Cinderella's breath caught in her chest. She looked to Lady Tremaine, who nodded sharply to get on with it before she and Anastasia took a seat. Cinderella took a deep breath and began:

> *"Starlight, moonlight.*
> *Sunrise, sunset.*
> *Each day is a new beginning,*
> *the bad ones we can forget.*
> *Look for sun, not for rain.*
> *Look for joy, not for pain."*

Lady Tremaine glanced around as Cinderella continued. The audience was captivated by the poem. As Cinderella recited the last line, Lady Tremaine started to stand. But to her surprise, Cinderella continued. It seemed as if she was making up stanzas right on the spot.

> *"Hands are for helping,*
> *not for harming.*
> *Speaking one's mind*

should not be alarming.
You can't steal joy
from one who strongly stands.
With hearts wide open,
happiness is in our hands."

The audience burst into applause. As she curtsied, Cinderella saw two ladies in the front row wipe tears from their eyes. She was proud of herself for speaking her mind, and for standing up for herself when her stepsisters had tried to keep her down. And for being brave enough to ask Lady Tremaine for exactly what she wanted. She smiled at everyone, moved by their support.

Cinderella turned to Anastasia as the ladies began exiting the music room. "Let's go check in on Drizella," she said.

Anastasia nodded sheepishly.

They found Drizella in her room, sulking in bed. She had changed into a nightgown and left Cinderella's dirty work dress in a pile on a chair—on top of Cinderella's missing dresses and clean apron.

"My clothes!" Cinderella said.

"Remove these dirty rags from this room at once," Anastasia ordered. "I can't imagine how they got here. You need to take better care of your things."

As Anastasia reached for the pile, Jaq and Perla came crawling out of a dress sleeve. "Ick! Mice!" she screamed, chucking the clothes at Cinderella.

Cinderella caught the pile, making sure Jaq and Perla were safely tucked away in the sleeve. She considered confronting her stepsisters about stealing her clothes. But as she watched Drizella pouting over missing her performance and Anastasia shuddering from her encounter with the mice, she figured they had already learned their lesson.

So instead she said, "Nice job today, Anastasia. And thank you, Drizella, for letting me borrow your dress. I'll return it after I've cleaned it." Then she walked out of the room with her head held high.

Once she was in the hallway, she unfolded the dress sleeve and coaxed her mouse friends out. "Come here, you two. Are you all right?"

"Of course, Cinderelly," Jaq said.

Perla held up the dress sleeve. "We found your missing clothes!"

Cinderella chuckled. "Thank you for being so brave, Perla."

"Cinderella," Lady Tremaine called down the hall. She had just said goodbye to the last guest.

Cinderella turned around, worried about what her stepmother had to say. She wouldn't be surprised if she was angry at her for performing alongside Anastasia. But it had been worth it.

"The ladies want to hear another poem from you during next month's salon," Lady Tremaine said flatly. "So be prepared."

"Yes, Stepmother," Cinderella said. "I promise I won't let you down."

Lady Tremaine walked away.

"You did it, Cinderelly!" Jaq said to Cinderella.

"We knew you could," Perla added.

Cinderella pulled a leftover cookie out of the pocket of Drizella's dress and handed it to the little mice.

"Good things come to those who are kind," Cinderella said as she smiled at her mouse friends. "I certainly know that to be true."

When has
YOUR
KINDNESS
helped someone?

MERIDA

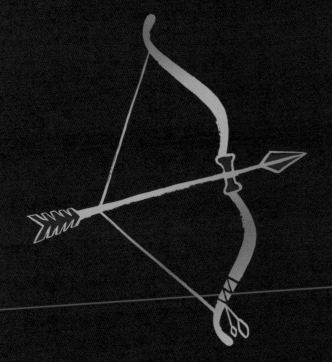

Determined to carve her own path in life, Merida defies an age-old custom sacred to the unruly and uproarious lords of the land. She believes it is possible to change her fate without compromising her values and integrity.

UNBEARABLE

WRITTEN BY SUDIPTA BARDHAN-QUALLEN & ILLUSTRATED BY SARA KIPIN

There is a legend about a princess of DunBroch named Merida who saved her kingdom from the demon bear, Mor'du. The princess broke the spell on Mor'du to free his spirit. She also broke a spell that was cast on her own mother, Queen Elinor, that had turned the queen into a bear. But there is more to this story than you think. There are more *bears* to this story—three more bears, to be precise. It all started as the Highland Games were about to begin.

Queen Elinor and King Fergus were busy making sure everything was ready for the clans to arrive. Elinor expected their daughter, Merida, to help. In fact, she expected a lot out of Merida. "Princesses must be responsible," Elinor said as they inspected the castle grounds.

Merida rolled her eyes. "Responsibility is boring," she muttered.

"Princesses don't mutter, either," Mum said.

Merida scowled.

The queen continued, "The other clans will be here soon. There are many things you have to learn before they get here. After all, a princess always strives for perfection."

"But I don't want to be perfect," Merida grumbled.

"Och," Mum said, frowning, "we cannot have this argument every day."

MERIDA IS . . .

CONFIDENT

REBELLIOUS

LOYAL

VALIANT

TRUE

DEDICATED

MERIDA'S DREAM:

To live life on her own terms

HEROIC MOMENT:

Fighting off Mor'du to save her mother and mend their bond

SIDEKICKS:

Harris, Hubert, and Hamish

FAMOUS QUOTE:

"Our fate lives within us. You only have to be brave enough to see it."

"I'll never be perfect, Mum!" Merida shouted. "I'll never be just like you!"

Elinor sighed. "Oh, Merida," she said. "The biggest part of perfection is doing the right thing. I know that's what you'll always do."

And the queen was right— Princess Merida *did* always want to do the right thing. It was just that Mum and Merida didn't always agree on what the right thing was. Which meant that, *sometimes*, they had disagreements. About when to wake up . . . and how to talk . . . and even what to wear.

Fergus said they argued because the queen and the princess were a lot more alike than they wished to admit. Merida wasn't sure about that.

It seemed as though Merida and Elinor were having even more disagreements than usual as the Highland Games grew closer. Then Merida found out that the clans were going to be presenting suitors to compete for the princess's hand in marriage. And her parents had agreed to this! She blamed her mother for the whole mess. If Elinor would just listen, Merida thought she could make her understand that she wasn't ready to get married. But the queen's mind was made up.

The day before the clans were going to arrive, the people of DunBroch gathered in the Great Hall of the castle. It was time to celebrate all the hard work and preparation they had completed.

As Fergus led the feast, Merida's three little brothers—the triplets—played one prank after another. When a head of cabbage rolled off a table, the boys began kicking it back and forth, creating a new game. Hubert accidentally kicked the cabbage and knocked Dad in the head. When he scowled at them, Hamish, Hubert, and Harris dashed out of the room.

"Go play kick the cabbage outside, you wee galoots!" Fergus roared. He tried to look fierce—except there was a cabbage leaf on his head. He looked so ridiculous that even Elinor began to giggle.

Everyone seemed to be laughing and having fun . . . except Merida. In fact, she needed to get away from the celebration—just for a little bit. She wandered toward the archery field, where she always felt better. But she discovered someone else there. It was a boy who was a bit older than Merida's brothers. He had a bow in his hands and was about to loose an arrow.

"Who are you?" Merida asked.

The boy misfired the arrow. It hit the target, but only at the very edge. Merida had clearly surprised him.

"Princess Merida!" the boy exclaimed.

"I'm sorry," Merida said. "I didn't mean to startle you."

The boy lowered his bow. "I'm Cullen," he said. "I hope it's all right that I'm out here."

"Of course it is," Merida replied. "Are you practicing for the competition?"

Cullen shook his head. "If I was older, I could compete. But my mum and dad say I'm too young." He frowned. "It's not fair that my parents get to decide what I'm allowed to do."

Merida snorted. "Och, I know! My parents are trying to make decisions for me, too."

"But you're a princess," Cullen said. "Don't you get to do whatever you want?"

"Ha!" Merida exclaimed. "Sometimes, I don't get to do *anything* I want!"

Out of the corner of her eye, Merida saw her brothers running toward her. They were still kicking the cabbage around. She waved, but they didn't wave back. She turned back to Cullen. "I know you can't compete officially," she said, "but if you'd like, we can have an archery contest right now."

Cullen's eyes grew wide. "That would be amazing!"

"Go ahead, then," Merida said. "You shoot first." She pointed to her brothers. "Just don't accidentally hit them!"

Cullen raised his bow again. He took aim. He scrunched his brows and concentrated. He looked so serious. Merida wanted to giggle, but she didn't want to hurt his feelings. She covered her mouth with her hand and waited for Cullen to shoot.

His arrow sailed through the air in a perfect arc. It hit the target just past the edge of the red bull's-eye.

"What a shot!" Merida said. She smiled. "That will be hard to beat."

Cullen beamed with happiness at the compliment, then said, "Your turn."

Merida faced the target and studied it. She drew her bow. She aimed. Just as she was about to loose the arrow . . . *THUMP!* A cabbage knocked into her elbow. "Michty me!" she exclaimed. Her arrow flew wildly and landed in the grass next to the target.

She turned and roared, "Boys! Which one of you did that?"

All three were holding toy swords. Hamish pointed his at Hubert. Hubert pointed his at Harris. Harris pointed his at Hamish.

Merida scowled. "Och!" she cried. "You boys are beasts! I wish all three of you would just be different!"

"Yeah!" Cullen agreed. "We're trying to have an archery contest. You're ruining it!"

The triplets hung their heads. They really hadn't meant to hit their sister. Now she was so angry! They didn't know what to do.

"Do you want to try again, Princess Merida?" Cullen asked. He held out one of his arrows for her to use.

But Merida was in too much of a bad mood now, even for archery. Besides, she had responsibilities to prepare for. Mum would certainly be looking for her. She scowled at her brothers again. "I have to get back to the castle now," she muttered.

"I'll come with you," Cullen said. He began to sling his bow over his shoulder.

Merida held up her hand to stop him. "I can't handle being around a bunch of babies," she said. She turned her back to leave before she

could see the look on Cullen's face. Her words had hurt him, and she didn't even realize.

Things didn't get better for Merida when the Highland Games began. As the legend tells, she won her own hand at the Highland Games. But that only created more fighting between Merida and Elinor. They had their worst argument ever, and by the end of it, Merida had left the castle in tears after slashing through their family tapestry. Angry and hurt, Merida wondered, *Why doesn't Mum understand? Or care?*

By the time Merida came back to DunBroch, she was ready to mend things with the queen. According to the legend, she was also ready to try to change her fate. While she was in the forest, Merida met a witch who gave her a magical cake. All she had to do was get Mum to eat it and everything about her life would change!

Merida eagerly served Mum the magical cake. "It's a peace offering," she said. "I made it. For you. Special."

Mum took a bite, just as Merida had planned. Unfortunately, nothing else went according to plan! Merida wanted to change Mum's mind about arranging her marriage, but the spell changed Mum's body—into that of a bear!

Merida needed to break the spell. She had to get Elinor-bear out of the castle and back to the Witch. And she had to do it before Dad found Elinor-bear. That meant someone had to distract Fergus. She needed someone who was smart, sly, and not afraid to make a little trouble. Merida needed help from . . . the triplets!

"A witch turned Mum into a bear. It's not my fault," Merida explained to her brothers. "We've got to get out of the castle. I need your help."

The boys distracted Fergus and the clansmen by creating a shadow bear. They tricked the men into going up to the roof and then locked them out.

Merida was very grateful. "I'll be back soon," Merida said as she snuck Elinor-bear out the kitchen door. "Go on and help yourself to anything you want, as a reward."

The kitchen was filled with goodies. But Merida barely looked back at her brothers, nor did she realize what she had left behind: the rest of the magical cake.

The boys noticed. They looked at each other. They looked at the cake on the table. It only had a tiny bite taken out of it. Merida had said they could have *anything*. . . .

Hamish went first. He broke off a small piece of the cake. He shoved it in his mouth and chewed. It tasted tart . . . and gamey . . . and delicious! He reached for another piece, but Hubert was too quick for him. He snatched the rest of the cake away.

Harris knew he had to move fast. The cake was moments away from disappearing into Hubert's mouth. He leaped forward and ripped a piece out of Hubert's hand. He was chewing before his feet even hit the ground.

All of a sudden, Hamish burped. He covered his mouth with his hand—except it wasn't a hand anymore. It was a paw! Hamish's mouth fell open. What was happening?

Hubert and Harris began to laugh. Their brother looked so silly with bear paws! But then Hubert burped, too. He quickly checked his hands. Luckily, they weren't paws. But there was something else wrong. Hubert's nose had become a bear snout!

Harris stopped laughing. One part-bear brother was funny. But two? That could be serious. He didn't know what was happening. He scratched his head to think . . . and noticed there were two new bumps. He checked his reflection in a pot. He had bear ears!

The boys didn't know what to say. But that didn't matter because, within moments, they couldn't talk at all—they could only growl. The triplets had turned into bears, just like Mum!

The triplets needed their sister. But she wasn't back from the forest yet. Fergus didn't like bears, so they couldn't risk being seen. They would have to hide until Merida came home.

Out in the forest, Merida and Elinor-bear weren't able to break the spell. But Merida thought she'd figured out what to do. The Witch had left a message for Merida: *Mend the bond torn by pride.* "The tapestry!" Merida guessed. She must need to sew up the tear in the family tapestry.

But sneaking back into a castle wasn't easy, especially when one of the people sneaking in was a giant bear. Merida and Elinor-bear made it inside—but then plans went awry. Elinor-bear fought her way out of the castle while Fergus locked Merida in the Tapestry Room for her own safety. "I'll not risk losing you!" he shouted.

Merida couldn't get Dad to listen to her. He didn't realize Elinor-bear was the queen! Time was running out. But Merida was still locked in. How would she open the lock?

Then Merida saw something through the peephole: bear cubs! Three *identical* bear cubs!

What had she done? Merida realized her brothers must have eaten the magical cake. But even before that, one foolish big sister had to *wish* for brothers who were different, the same way she had wished for a mother who was different.

Merida knew she'd have to apologize to the triplets—but it would have to wait. *Right now,* she thought, *I need their help. I have to get out of here and help Mum!* She looked right at her bear brothers. "Get the key!" she said.

Inside the Tapestry Room, Merida pulled the family tapestry off the wall. She began to sew up the tear. But she didn't have enough time to finish mending it. As boys or as bears, it didn't take long for the triplets to race back and toss the key to their sister.

"Thank you, boys," Merida said, unlocking the door. She grabbed the tapestry and the needle and thread, then ran down the stairs. The cubs followed her. But Merida stopped and shook her head. "No, boys, no," she said. "You three stay here. This tapestry will break the spell. I have to get it to Mum before Dad finds her."

The triplets still wanted to help. Elinor-bear was their mother, too! They had to show Merida how brave they could be.

Hamish-bear climbed on Hubert-bear's shoulders. Hubert-bear climbed on Harris-bear's shoulders. Then the triple stack of bears roared all at once.

But Merida just frowned. "It's too dangerous," she said. "I don't have time for three wee babies." She pointed to the staircase. "Now go back upstairs and wait for me. I'll be back soon."

The disappointed cubs shuffled up the stairs, barely paying attention to anything. They didn't even know anyone was behind them until they heard someone shout, "I've got you!"

Merida turned, hearing the shout. *Should I go check on the boys?* she wondered. *But what about Mum?* She couldn't waste any time!

She heard growling, then whimpers. A voice called, "I'm going to make trophies out of you three, just like King Fergus does with the bears he captures!"

Merida bit her lip. She didn't usually worry about her brothers. Those boys could handle anything. But at the moment, they weren't *boys. I didn't pay attention to the triplets,* Merida thought, *and they got turned into bears. If I don't pay attention to them now, who knows what will happen?*

That's when Merida knew she had to do the right thing. Mum wouldn't want her to leave the triplets in any kind of danger. She dropped the tapestry and ran toward the noises.

When Merida reached the top of the stairs, she saw Cullen standing in front of the boy-cubs. He was pointing a pitchfork at them. The cubs looked terrified.

"Cullen!" Merida shouted. She rushed toward him. "What are you doing?"

"I found bears!" Cullen replied, grinning. "My father said I was too young to help. But he was wrong! I'm protecting everyone!"

"Protecting?" Merida asked. She stepped between Cullen and the cubs, pushing the boys behind her to shield them. "Protecting from what? From three wee babies?"

Cullen frowned. "All the men in the land are out hunting bears. But they didn't even know about these animals!" He poked the pitchfork toward the cubs and then pointed at his own chest. "I'm the only one who can defend the clans against these monsters!"

"But, Cullen," Merida said, "you can only defend someone if there is danger. Look at these cubs." She pointed at the triplets. "They can't hurt you. You don't need to be scared of them."

"I'm not scared!" Cullen snapped.

Merida frowned. She could tell the boy was getting upset. Trying to talk to someone who was feeling out of sorts could make everything worse, so Merida had to calm Cullen down first. "Of course you're not scared," she said. "Because bear cubs aren't anything to be scared of." She pulled Cullen closer to the bear cubs so he could stand next to them. "You're clearly bigger and stronger than all three of these cubs put together," she continued. "Going out of your way to hurt others who are weaker than you is *not* doing the right thing."

"They're just animals," Cullen mumbled. But he lowered the pitchfork, too.

"Animals deserve kindness and love like any other living thing," Merida said. "You don't know anything about these cubs. They're clearly afraid to be away from their mother. They need your compassion, not to be treated with cruelty."

Cullen looked down at the floor. "I didn't think about that," he said. "I didn't mean to be cruel, I promise. Everyone thinks I'm too little to do anything good. But I'm not too little."

Merida gulped. She remembered calling her brothers and Cullen babies. She realized how much that must have hurt.

"I was just trying to do the right thing," Cullen said.

Merida saw tears splash on Cullen's shoes. She sighed. She had to do the right thing again.

"Cullen," Merida said. She knelt down so she could look the boy in the eye. "I owe you an apology."

"What?" Cullen asked, sniffling. He wiped his eyes. "I'm the one who was wrong."

Merida put her hands on Cullen's shoulders. "We were both wrong," she said. "You didn't think about how your actions made the cubs feel. But I didn't think about how *my* actions made *you* feel. And I'm very sorry about that." She smiled. "You and I are a lot alike," she said. "We both needed a reminder about being kind and compassionate to others instead of just thinking about ourselves."

"That isn't always easy to do," Cullen said.

Merida shook her head. "No, it's not," she said. "Especially when you are feeling hurt yourself. You helped me learn that I shouldn't use my own hurt as an excuse to ignore someone else's feelings." She looked over at the cubs. "Or to ignore some other bear's feelings!"

The cubs nodded in agreement.

"You and I are alike in another way, too, Cullen," Merida continued. "We both try to do the right thing. That means we both have work to do right now."

Cullen frowned. "What?" he asked.

Merida smiled. "I'm going to take these cubs back out to the forest. With luck, they'll be able to find their mother." She quickly winked at the triplets. "My father and the lords are in the forest right now. They might get back to Castle DunBroch before I do. If you see him, it would really help if you could make sure my father knows I'm safe and I'll be home soon. Tonight has been scary enough. I don't want him to worry about me!"

Cullen grinned and nodded. "You can count on me, Princess Merida!" He ran off to keep watch at the castle gates. Merida knew that she could trust him to be responsible.

When Cullen was gone, Merida gathered up the tapestry again.

She looked at the triplets. "Well, boys," she said, "we need to get moving! You three beasts had better come with me."

The bear cubs grinned. Merida climbed into her horse's saddle and held out her hand. She pulled her bear brothers up one at a time. "Hold on tight!" she exclaimed. Soon they were all racing through the forest. They heard the dogs barking as the warriors chased after Elinor-bear. The cubs trembled with fear. But Merida said,

> "I've seen you three
> be very BRAVE.
> If we WORK TOGETHER,
> I know we can save Mum."

The cubs nodded. Merida was right! In fact, they figured, she probably wouldn't be able to save *anything* without their help!

It wasn't easy, but Merida managed to reach Elinor-bear in time and break the spell. When Elinor became human, the triplets transformed, too. Merida had her family back!

Of course, the magic didn't disappear completely. As legend says, after spending some time as bears, the triplets were a bit *wilder* than they had been before. But Merida didn't mind. "You might be un*bear*able, boys," she said, "but you're the perfect brothers for me!"

When have you HELPED someone IN NEED?

SNOW
WHITE

She's been called "the fairest one of all," but Snow White is best known for her kindness to all living things, her loving nature, and her sweet voice. Ever optimistic, she makes the best of any situation. Even though she must leave the castle to flee her wicked stepmother, she makes a happy home with her new dwarf friends. And when she's most afraid, she knows that a smile and a song will make everything better.

AFTER THE STORM

WRITTEN BY ERIN FALLIGANT & ILLUSTRATED BY NATHANNA ÉRICA

*P*link, *plink, plink!*
As the first raindrops splattered off the cottage window, Snow White peered outside. Dark, sinister clouds loomed overhead. The Seven Dwarfs were late coming home from work at the diamond mine. Would they get caught in the storm?

Snow White pulled her cape over her head and hurried outside. She searched the shadowy woods beneath the dark sky. She called out the Dwarfs' names one by one, hoping to hear their reply. Finally, she heard the whistles of a familiar song in the distance. The Dwarfs were coming!

"Thank goodness!" Snow White cried—just as the clouds burst overhead. Rain pelted down, soaking her cape and splashing into the stream beneath the wooden bridge.

Snow White tightened her hood. "Oh, please hurry!" she called toward the Dwarfs. High above her, the wind moaned and tree branches groaned.

At last, Snow White saw a lantern bobbing through the trees. Doc led the way, with the other six dwarfs marching close behind. They sloshed along the muddy trail, the handles of their pickaxes bobbing on their shoulders.

"Quickly now!" Snow White called to them from the bridge. "Come on inside!"

SNOW WHITE IS . . .

CAREFREE
EMPATHETIC
COMFORTING
SWEET
LOVING
POSITIVE

SNOW WHITE'S DREAM:

To fill the world with sunshine

HEROIC MOMENT:

Pushing past her fears to build a new life for herself

SIDEKICKS:

the Seven Dwarfs

FAMOUS QUOTE:

"I'm sure I'll get along somehow. Everything's going to be all right."

But just as the Dwarfs were crossing the bridge . . .

Crack! Lightning lit up the sky.

Boom! Thunder roared.

Creak! A tree began to fall toward the Dwarfs' cottage.

Crash! The thatched roof of the cottage split in two.

Snow White gasped. When she had escaped from her evil stepmother into the forest, the Dwarfs' cottage had become her new home.

"I knew it!" cried Grumpy. "I've been warning you all for years that one of those old trees was going to come down."

Doc wiped the raindrops from his glasses and looked again at the cottage. "Doh *ear*!" he said. "I mean, oh dear! What now?"

As another bolt of lightning streaked across the sky, Snow White found her voice. "Now we go inside," she said firmly. "We can't be out here during the storm."

"B-but . . . what about the tree?" whispered Bashful. He twisted his beard side to side.

"Everything will be all right," said Snow White. "We'll find a cozy corner where we can stay warm and dry. We'll be safe." But as she led the Dwarfs to the cottage door, her stomach fluttered. What would they find inside?

The front door creaked open, and a frightened bluebird flew out.

"Oh, poor thing," said Snow White. "Was your home destroyed in the storm?"

The bluebird whistled frantically before disappearing into the darkness.

"It appears *our* home was destroyed, too," said Happy, whose jolly smile had been replaced by a frown. He pointed toward the kitchen, where the tree rested across a broken kitchen table, broken chairs, and a broken hutch. Pots and pans were scattered across the floor among rain puddles.

As they inspected the fallen tree inside the cottage, Snow White saw an abandoned bird's nest dangling from a broken branch. A few soft blue feathers were woven into the twigs. "Oh my," she said. "I hope that little bluebird will find a safe place to sleep tonight." She cradled the nest in her hands and placed it on a stool by the door.

"Everything is ruined," muttered Grumpy. He crossed his arms.

"Well, now, not *everything*," said Snow White in her cheeriest voice. "The tree only fell in the kitchen. Let's close the shutters. Hurry now!"

"But this one's broken!" said Sneezy, pointing to a cracked panel that dangled from its hinge. As the wind blew in through the open window, his nose twitched. *"Achoo!"* His sneeze blew the other shutter closed.

"Bless you!" said Snow White. "Leave the broken shutters and close the ones you can."

Working together, they closed every shutter that wasn't broken. *Boom! Ba-boom, boom!*

Thunder roared overhead, sending Snow White's heart racing. But when she noticed Dopey shaking beside her, she kept her voice steady. "Let's find a dry place to wait out the storm," she said. "Here, by the organ. Come now—sit with me."

She took off her wet cape and settled onto the floor, wrapping her arms around the Dwarfs. "How shall we pass the time?" she asked.

"I know!" said Doc, raising his finger in the air. "We could bead a rook—er, I mean, read a book!" But as he headed toward the bookshelf, he stopped. "Oh, dear. The shelf is destroyed." He picked up a dripping wet book and fanned the pages, trying to dry them out.

Sleepy yawned. "We could go to bed," he suggested. But as he started up the staircase, lightning cracked and the wind howled through the hole in the roof above. Sleepy's eyes widened. "Or maybe we could sleep down here." He curled up on a tiny bench.

"Surely there must be something else we can do," Snow White said. "How about some music?"

Dopey nudged Grumpy and pointed toward the organ.

"You want me to play a song?" said Grumpy. "Well, I can't. I'll bet that organ is ruined, too."

Dopey jumped up and played a few keys, just to prove that it *wasn't.* But the stool that Grumpy usually sat on was partially hidden beneath the tree's branches. Dopey tugged and tugged, and when he finally managed to pull the stool out, his shoulders slumped. It was split in two.

"Meh, it wasn't that comfortable anyway," Grumpy muttered, though Snow White could see a little sadness in his eyes. "See?" he continued. "I told you. Everything is ruined. *And* there's nothing to do."

Snow White forced a smile. "I have an idea," she said. "What do we do when things go wrong?"

Bashful whispered in her ear.

"That's right!" she said. "We sing a song. Let's see now . . . I think I know the perfect one." She gathered the Dwarfs toward her and began to sing in her sweet, soothing voice.

> *"A little complaining won't stop clouds from raining*
> *When storms fill the sky overhead.*
> *There's no use in hiding when you're feeling frightened.*
> *Just comfort a good friend instead."*

As Snow White sang, her own fears melted away. Eventually, the howling wind died down. The rain slowed to a pitter-patter. And Sleepy's soft snoring filled the cozy corner.

The other dwarfs began to drift off to sleep, one by one. Soon Snow White felt sleepy, too. She yawned and closed her eyes.

When she awoke, sunlight streamed down through the hole in the roof.

"Good morning," Snow White said as the Dwarfs stretched around her.

"What time is it?" Sleepy asked, rubbing his eyes.

Just then, the cuckoo clock struck seven. The wooden squirrel rang its bell and the wooden frog emerged from the doors of the clock, ready to croak seven times. But only the tiniest *peep* came out. The clock was broken, too!

Dopey hopped up to slide a finger down a long crack that ran through the center of the clock. His hat slipped down over his eyes.

"Even the frog has lost its croak!" Grumpy huffed. "What did I tell you? Ruined. All of it. And *what* will we do about *that*?" He wagged his finger at the tree that had taken over their cottage.

Snow White sighed. "We'll have to make the best of it," she said. "I know! I'll bet we could use the wood from that tree to repair the roof and build new furniture."

"Why, yes!" said Happy, his cheeks aglow. "Starting with a new kitchen table. A wider one that can hold more breakfast dishes." He smiled at the thought, and his stomach rumbled.

Sleepy stretched, still trying to get comfortable on the tiny bench. "Or we could build a longer bench," he said with a yawn.

"Nonsense!" said Grumpy. "We should make everything *exactly* the way it was before."

"Except the bookshelf," said Doc, staring at the books on the floor. "We should build that taller, to hold more books!"

"We should make the shutters thicker, to keep the dust out," Sneezy said. As he opened the shutters to let in the morning light, his nose twitched. "*Achoo!*"

Grumpy held up his hands to avoid the blast. "No, no, no!" he said, stomping his foot. "There's not enough wood. Like I said, we should make everything *exactly* the way it was before."

"There now," said Snow White. "We needn't argue. There's plenty of wood for all of your wishes." She eyed the tree's thick trunk and its knotted branches. "We could make the kitchen table a little wider, the bench a few inches longer, the bookshelf one shelf taller, and the shutters slightly thicker."

All the Dwarfs nodded in unison as she went through the list— well, all except Grumpy.

Snow White chuckled. "I'll bet we could make something for each one of you! Grumpy, what do you wish for? Dopey and Bashful, do you have wishes, too?"

Dopey stared up at the cuckoo clock. He pointed at the wooden frog, which was stuck outside the clock's tiny doors.

"Would you like to give the frog its croak back?" asked Snow White.

When he nodded, she smiled and patted his shoulder. "I'm sure there'll be plenty of wood for that."

Bashful picked up a bouquet of wildflowers that had fallen from a broken windowsill. Then he whispered something in Happy's ear.

"Bashful would like sturdier windowsills," said Happy. "To hold more flowers for Snow White."

"Bashful, how sweet," said Snow White. She kissed his head.

"Oh, gosh," he said, his cheeks flushing red.

"Now how about you, Grumpy?" Snow White asked again. "There must be *something* you're wishing for."

Grumpy crossed his arms. "Nope!"

Snow White gazed around the cottage. "I know! How about a new stool for your organ? We could make it *exactly* the same as the old one."

Grumpy shrugged.

"Or maybe," she added, "we could make the seat a bit softer. I could sew you a feather pillow for it. Wouldn't that be nice?"

Grumpy opened his mouth to argue but then closed it.

When he didn't grumble, Snow White clapped her hands. "It's settled, then! We can use the tree to repair the cottage and to make everything just a bit better."

They got to work right away. The Dwarfs used their pickaxes to chop up the tree while Snow White sanded and smoothed the wood. To fix the roof, the Dwarfs stood on each other's shoulders to reach the highest rafters as Snow White helped hammer the new boards in place.

Together, they built a kitchen table that was a little wider. A bench that was a few inches longer. A bookshelf that was one shelf taller. Shutters that were slightly thicker. A cuckoo clock that croaked a touch louder. And windowsills that were a bit sturdier.

Snow White sewed a tiny feather pillow for Grumpy's new organ stool to make it more comfortable. As she placed it on the seat, Grumpy's mouth twitched into an almost smile.

"There!" she announced. "We're finished."

The Dwarfs cheered and tried out their new creations.

"You were right," said Doc as he placed the last book on the shelf. "There was plenty of wood for all our wishes. And there's even a bit left over!" He pointed at the scraps of wood resting by the door.

Snow White smiled. "Of course there is," she said.

"There's always ENOUGH to go around, if we SHARE."

"The cottage looks better than ever, with special things for each one of you."

"Except for you!" Bashful said out loud. He clapped his hand over his mouth, as if frightened by the sound of his own voice.

"Oh, dear," said Doc. "Rashful is bright. No, no . . . I mean, Bashful is right! We forgot to give *you* a wish, Snow White!"

She wrapped the Dwarfs in a hug. "You're such dears," she said. "But I have everything I need right here." At that moment, she was perfectly happy. She wanted only dinner and a cozy bed.

"Let's get washed up," Doc said to the other dwarfs. "Snow White, you rest your feet while I start a kettle of soup on the hearth."

A short while later, Doc served hot soup to the Dwarfs and Snow White, who were lined up along their new table. After dinner, Sneezy closed the new shutters and Bashful arranged a fresh bouquet of wildflowers on the new sill.

When it was time for bed, Snow White helped Doc reach a bedtime book from the new bookshelf. Grumpy played a lullaby on the organ, sitting comfortably on his feather pillow. Sleepy stretched out along the new bench and drifted off to sleep. And when the new cuckoo clock struck nine, Dopey smiled up at the croaking frog. He crouched low and happily hopped across the floor like a frog—until he crashed into Grumpy.

"All right, now," said Snow White with a laugh. "Off to bed with you."

Once all the Dwarfs were tucked in, she crawled into her bed and fell into a deep, happy sleep.

Snow White slept so peacefully that she didn't hear the Seven Dwarfs get back out of bed. She didn't hear them tiptoe downstairs and gather the last bits of wood from the fallen tree. She didn't hear them carry the wood outside, where they spent the night carving a special surprise for her.

When she awoke the next morning, the cottage was quiet. "Hello?" she called. "Where has everyone gone?" Had the Dwarfs left for work without saying goodbye?

She pulled on her cloak and hurried outside. "Hello?"

Dopey popped around the corner of the cottage wearing a goofy smile. He waved his arm for her to follow. Then he raised his finger to his lips, as if guarding a secret, and began to tiptoe back around the house.

"What is it, Dopey?" Snow White asked. She gathered her skirt and hurried after him.

When she rounded the corner, she saw the other six dwarfs standing along the river that ran past the cottage. Their cheeks were flushed with excitement. Even Grumpy looked a little *less* grumpy.

"Whatever is going on?" she asked with a laugh.

"Come with us," said Happy as the Dwarfs led her to a pretty little waterfall downstream. Overhead, a sheet had been draped over a tree branch.

"Surprise!" announced the Dwarfs. They pulled the sheet away to reveal a handsome new sign hanging from the branch next to the waterfall. Snow White stepped closer to read the words: *Snow White's Wishing Waterfall*.

"Oh my goodness," she said. "You did this for me?" Happy tears welled up in her eyes.

"Now you'll be able to wake a mish—er, I mean, make a wish!" said Doc.

"*Lots* of wishes!" whispered Bashful. "It was Grumpy's idea."

When Snow White turned toward Grumpy, he blushed. "Now don't you go getting all mushy," he said. But when she bent low to kiss his head, he didn't pull away.

"We used the last of the wood from the fallen tree," said Happy, smiling wide. "Well, almost. There's just one piece left." He lifted a long board that was leaning against the tree trunk.

"What should we do with the last piece of woo—" Sneezy broke off and wound up for a sneeze, but Dopey jumped in and held a finger under his nose. "Thank you," he said before continuing. "The last piece of—*achoo!*"

"Bless you," Snow White said. She studied the piece of wood.

Just then, the bluebird landed on the tree branch. Snow White gasped. "I'll be right back!" she called as she ran toward the cottage.

Moments later, Snow White returned holding the little nest. "We'll build a birdhouse for the bluebird's nest!" she announced. The Dwarfs nodded in agreement.

Once the birdhouse was hung from the branch and the bluebird and his nest were nestled cozily inside, Dopey tugged on Snow White's skirt. He pointed toward the sign.

"What is it, Dopey?" she asked. "Oh, do you want me to make a wish?"

Dopey nodded so hard he nearly fell over.

"Well, all right. Let's see now. . . ." Snow White stepped toward the waterfall, picked up a smooth pebble, and closed her eyes. Her wishes for the future swirled through her mind: adventures in faraway places, joyful meals with her dwarf friends, courage for future storms. But when she opened one eye, she saw all seven dwarfs standing beside her with pebbles in their hands, closing their eyes tightly, too. So she made a new wish.

"I wish for . . . sunshine," she said. "No more storms for a good long while. Only sunshine." She tossed the little stone into the waterfall.

As soon as she'd made the wish, each dwarf flicked his pebble into the waterfall, echoing the word "sunshine." Even Grumpy added his wish, though he grumbled something under his breath about how sunshine was overrated.

The bluebird twittered in gratitude.

Snow White smiled. "Thank you for my wishing waterfall," she said to the Dwarfs. "Now we'll *always* have plenty of wishes."

Happy's stomach rumbled so loudly that even Bashful blushed.

Snow White laughed. "Don't worry, Happy. There'll be plenty of breakfast, too. Come back inside."

As she led the Seven Dwarfs into the cottage, the morning sun peeked out from behind a cloud—another wish come true.

How can YOU make WISHES come true?

RAPUNZEL

Rapunzel is creative, fun-loving, friendly, and brave. She once had magical hair that glowed when she sang a special song and could heal any ailment, including old age. For eighteen years, Rapunzel had one dream: to see the lanterns that rose into the air every year on her birthday. By stepping out of her comfort zone, Rapunzel finally made that dream come true—and learned that she was the kingdom's lost princess. Now, back home with her family, it's time for Rapunzel to find a new dream.

STARRY-EYED QUEST

WRITTEN BY KATHY MCCULLOUGH & ILLUSTRATED BY NICOLETTA BALDARI

Rapunzel gazed out at the dazzling night sky above her. Up on the castle roof, there was nothing to block her view. "Look, Pascal!" she told the little chameleon on her shoulder. "The stars seem to go on for days—days and nights!" Pascal raised a sleepy head and nodded, then went back to his nap.

Since escaping the tower and returning home to the castle, Rapunzel couldn't get enough of the view. She'd quickly figured out the rear side of the roof was the best for stargazing. It was the highest and darkest spot in the kingdom.

Eugene emerged from the doorway onto the roof to join her. "Aren't the stars beautiful?" Rapunzel asked him, lifting her arm up toward the sky. Without the glow of the moon to hide the most distant stars, it seemed as if an extra sweep of sparkling silver dust had been painted over the sky.

Eugene nodded and laughed. "Sure," he said. "But you say that every night. They're the same stars as yesterday—*and* the day before."

"But the view is different every night!" Rapunzel pointed to a constellation of bright stars directly above them. "Orion has moved a little to the east. See? And now Taurus is in front of us. Right there."

Growing up, Rapunzel had only been able to see the part of the night sky visible through the tower's single window. But this unchanging view had helped her learn how to track the path of the stars through

RAPUNZEL IS . . .

INDEPENDENT
ADVENTUROUS
IMAGINATIVE
OPEN
INQUISITIVE
ENTHUSIASTIC

RAPUNZEL'S DREAM:

Using kindness to light up
the world

HEROIC MOMENT:

Escaping the tower

SIDEKICK:

Pascal

FAMOUS QUOTE:

"No, I will not stop. For every
minute of the rest of my life,
I will fight."

the seasons. Of the three textbooks Mother Gothel had given her in the tower, the astronomy book had been the first one Rapunzel memorized. She'd even drawn a star map on the tower ceiling.

"You don't know how lucky you are!" Rapunzel told Eugene. "You've been able to look up at all of this, anytime, your whole life."

Eugene shrugged. "In the forest, there are trees overhead, remember," he said. "Plus, moonless nights were the best nights for thieving. We weren't paying much attention to the stars."

Before Eugene had met Rapunzel, he'd been a bandit known as Flynn Rider. He had first encountered Rapunzel when he'd snuck into the tower to hide from the royal guard. Later, he'd helped her with her escape.

"You're not a thief anymore," Rapunzel pointed out. "Now you can enjoy the night sky whenever you want!"

"No one could ever enjoy the stars as much as *you*, Rapunzel," Eugene said with a grin.

Rapunzel smiled. She plucked Pascal off her shoulder and held him over her head. "Look, Pascal! Out there somewhere might be a constellation shaped like a chameleon! If I could find it, I'd name it after you!"

Pascal let out an excited squeak.

Rapunzel raised the telescope she'd brought home with her from the tower. Through the telescope's lens, the silver dust twinkled brighter, but the stars were still tiny and distant. "I wish I could see them even better!" She lowered the telescope with a frown.

"Can you buy a bigger telescope?" Eugene asked.

"I'd need a *huge* telescope to see those tiny stars," Rapunzel replied. "The kind they have in observatories." She knew from her astronomy book that an observatory's giant telescope was at least ten times as long as the one in her hand, and its magnifying lens was ten times as wide. That's why an observatory telescope needed a whole building to hold it.

"There's an observatory in Stellonia," Eugene said. "Greno pointed it out to me once." Greno was one of the "pub thugs," former bandits like Eugene. They, too, had given up their thieving ways after being inspired by Rapunzel to follow their dreams.

"I read about that observatory in my book!" Rapunzel said. "But it's not close enough to visit every night."

"You'd need an observatory here in the kingdom for that," Eugene said. "Last I checked, we don't have one."

A smile spread over Rapunzel's face. "Not *yet*," she said.

Rapunzel explained to her parents that the observatory wouldn't be just for her, but for the whole kingdom to share. The King and Queen were delighted with the idea. They arranged for Rapunzel to meet with the royal architects, who were thrilled with the assignment. Finally, something more challenging to work on than a storage shed or castle wall repair! They combed through the observatory designs in the books Rapunzel brought them from the royal library. Within days, they had a blueprint ready.

Meanwhile, Rapunzel hired bricklayers and builders from the village. When the pub thugs found out about the project, they arrived at the castle to help as well. Attila, who now ran a bakery, brought pastries for the crew. "You inspired us to live *our* dreams," Attila told Rapunzel as he offered her a walnut roll. "The least we can do is help you live yours."

"It sure will be nice to see old Pegasus up close again," Greno said as he slathered mortar onto a brick.

"Again?" Rapunzel asked, surprised Greno knew about the horse-shaped constellation.

Greno pointed to the tattoo of a circled star on his left arm. "Amateur astronomer. That's *my* dream." He smiled. "I used to visit the Stellonia Observatory whenever I was in the area. Augustine Salvari took me under his wing and taught me all about the constellations."

"You know Augustine Salvari?" Rapunzel said. Now she was even more amazed. She'd read all about the famous lens maker. "He made the telescope lenses for the Stellonia Observatory! We should ask him to make ours!"

Rapunzel had found local ironsmiths to build the casing for the observatory's giant telescope, but the one lens maker in the kingdom knew how to make only spectacles. He'd succeeded in creating the eyepiece for the small end of the telescope, but his attempts at the larger lens had been failures.

Greno shook his head. "Augustine lost his sight a few years ago and had to retire," he said. "He barely comes out of his cottage. He doesn't even like talking about the stars anymore. He's given up on his dream."

Rapunzel tried to imagine what it would be like not to see the stars again. Not to see her parents' faces, her new home in the kingdom, Eugene's goofy grin, or Pascal's big brown eyes and cute little tail . . .

Would she want to hide from the world? Maybe. For a while, anyway. But the things she couldn't see would still be out there, and she hoped she'd find *some* way to connect with them again—the way books had connected her to the outside world when she was trapped in the tower.

"Maybe we can inspire him to dream again," Rapunzel said. "We should at least try."

A few days later, Rapunzel arrived outside Augustine's small vine-covered cottage with Greno. Before she could even knock, a gruff voice called out from inside. "Is that you, Greno? It's about time! I'm all out of walnut rolls!"

Rapunzel smiled and held up a box. "Should I tell him we brought gifts?" she whispered. She had learned from Greno about Augustine's love of Attila's baked goods.

"Is someone out there with you?" Augustine asked. He might not have been able to see well anymore, but his hearing was as sharp as ever. "Go away!" he barked.

"It's just me, Rapunzel," Rapunzel said through the door. "I'm so sorry to bother you, but we're building an observatory here in the kingdom. We need your help to make the large lens for the telescope."

"*Princess* Rapunzel?" Augustine said. "It's an honor to have you visit me, of course. But didn't Greno tell you I'm blind?" His voice was now more sad than gruff. "I'm sorry . . . I can't help you."

"But you can!" Rapunzel said. "Our lens maker has never made a large telescope lens before. You could guide him."

After a moment, the cottage door creaked open, revealing a hunched, bearded man in a long, tattered blue robe. He seemed to stare straight at her, but his dark eyes were cloudy and blank. Rapunzel could see the sadness in them. "Why should I help build a telescope I'll never be able to use?" he asked her.

Rapunzel hesitated. She didn't want to say anything that might add to Augustine's sadness. She felt afraid—but it was a different kind of fear from what she'd felt while fleeing from the tower with Eugene. She needed a different type of courage—the kind that came from the heart.

"Do you know my story, about growing up trapped in a tower?" Rapunzel asked.

Augustine nodded, and Rapunzel continued.

"There were times I was afraid I'd never be free," she said. "But every night I wished on a star." She paused, gazing at the sky.

"There were so MANY STARS, I knew I could *never* run out of WISHES. That gave me HOPE."

"I wished on stars when I was young, too," Augustine said. "My wish was to learn how to build a telescope to find the stars *beyond* the stars I wished on."

"And your wish came true!" Rapunzel said. "Think of how many people have looked through your telescope in Stellonia and learned there's more to the night sky than they've ever dreamed. The telescope you help make for our new observatory would show even *more* people!"

Augustine grew quiet. "That does seem like a worthy project," he said at last.

"Then you'll help us?" Rapunzel asked.

Augustine clapped his hands and smiled. "What are we waiting for? Let's get to work!"

"Thank you so much!" Rapunzel said. "But before we go—how about a walnut roll?" She opened the box of pastries. Greno handed Augustine the stickiest roll. Augustine's face lit up at the smell, and he started eating.

Rapunzel shared a happy look with Greno. They had their master lens maker!

Rapunzel set up a workshop for Augustine at the castle where he could instruct the local lens maker in creating the giant telescope lens. She made sure Attila kept them supplied with plenty of fresh walnut rolls.

Once the builders and pub thugs had finished the new observatory walls, Rapunzel decorated them with paintings of the night sky. She labeled each of the stars, constellations, and planets so the visitors would know what they were.

Most evenings, Rapunzel invited Augustine to join her on the castle roof with Eugene and Greno. Pascal often sat on Augustine's shoulder. The lens maker's long white hair was very soft and made an excellent place for napping.

"Cepheus is just above us," Rapunzel told Augustine. "Ursa Major is straight ahead."

"So Ursa Minor would be just about there!" Augustine pointed to a collection of stars between the other two constellations Rapunzel had named.

"That's right!" Rapunzel said.

Greno elbowed Eugene. "How about you, Eugene? See anything you recognize?" Greno and Rapunzel had been teaching Eugene using the constellation paintings on the observatory wall.

"I see . . ." Eugene grinned at the snoozing Pascal. "The Napping Chameleon!"

Pascal perked up at this. Rapunzel laughed. "He's joking," she told Pascal.

"There *is* a chameleon constellation, though," Augustine said. "You can only see it in the night sky from the southern hemisphere. Very far away. I saw it once, at an observatory south of the equator." Augustine lifted Pascal off his shoulder, holding him upside down. "It has four stars for the body"—Augustine tapped Pascal's back, outlining where the stars would be—"and three for the tail." He stretched Pascal's tail upward.

Pascal clutched Augustine's arm with his forelegs. Having his own constellation was nice, but he wasn't sure he'd like hanging upside down in the sky forever.

Augustine set Pascal back on his shoulder. "I only wish I could touch the stars, too," he said.

Rapunzel watched as Augustine patted Pascal's head. A thought occurred to her. "Maybe you *could*, though," she said as the idea took shape in her mind.

Augustine laughed. "The stars are a bit too far away, Your Highness. That's why we're making the telescope."

Rapunzel patted his shoulder fondly. She had a surprise in store for her friend Augustine.

Soon the telescope was at last complete, its magnifying lens in place. The observatory was ready to open!

"Welcome to the Royal Observatory," Rapunzel announced as she opened the doors. She was thrilled to see the villagers lined up to visit, just as she had hoped. "Come in, come in!"

Rapunzel and Augustine led the visitors through the building, explaining which of the planets and constellations on the wall they would be able to see through the telescope once the sun had set. Greno signed students up for astronomy classes, and Eugene helped out at an arts and crafts table. He even let the young artists make him into a model of the solar system by hanging their handmade planets from his arms.

Rapunzel glanced around at the happy scene. She spotted her parents listening closely as Augustine told them the history behind the different constellations, and saw Greno teaching his fellow pub thugs how stars helped sailors navigate the seas.

Rapunzel smiled to herself. Her dream had been to build this observatory—and that dream had come true, but in a way that surprised her. She hadn't even looked through the new telescope yet, but what she saw around her made her as happy as any stars ever could.

A little later, Rapunzel took Augustine aside and told him she had a gift for him. "This is a book of maps you can 'see' with your fingers," Rapunzel said, placing the gift in his hands. "I made clay templates of different areas of the sky, with tiny sculpted dots for the stars," she explained. "I pressed damp paper over them, and when the paper dried, the stars stayed raised off the paper!"

Augustine nodded to himself. "With the stars raised up off of the surface . . . I can *see* them through touch."

Rapunzel held open the book and Augustine brushed his fingers over one of the finished maps. "Ah! Leo!" he said as he touched the stars that made up a constellation in the shape of a lion's head. He moved on to a snakelike line of stars. "Hydra . . ." His smile grew bigger with each new constellation. "Here's Cancer the crab!" He reached out to place both hands on the map. "This is amazing!"

Augustine closed the book and held it close. "Thanks to you, I can look at the stars every night!" he told Rapunzel.

She smiled. She was so happy to have helped Augustine bring his dream alive again.

When it finally got dark enough, the visitors lined up at the telescope. Rapunzel insisted on waiting until everyone else had their turn. She stood a few feet away, watching the villagers and others ooh and aah as they peered through the telescope at the stars.

Eugene joined Rapunzel. "I've never seen you be this patient about *anything*," he told her.

"I can be patient," Rapunzel protested. "Sometimes."

Eugene laughed.

After the last of the visitors had gone, only Eugene and Rapunzel were left. Rapunzel gestured for Eugene to look first. He squinted through the lens. "Uh-oh. It's gotten cloudy," he said.

"What? No!" Rapunzel said. She noticed the grin on Eugene's face. "That's *not* funny," she said.

She took her place at the telescope, nervous and excited. Would it be as amazing as she hoped? She leaned in to peer through the lens—and gasped. "Oh, Eugene! It's so beautiful."

"It is," he agreed.

Through the telescope's lens, stars and planets, and swirls of gas and dust, glittered and glowed. "The stars that were so far away— they seem so much closer!" she said. "But now I can see even *more* stars, even farther away. I want to see *those* stars up close, too!"

Eugene laughed. "Too bad you can't *fly* up there." He noticed a thoughtful look spread over Rapunzel's face. "I'm joking," he said. "What are you going to do? Build a rocket?"

Rapunzel smiled at Eugene. "Why not?" she said. "The stars have a way of making *anything* seem possible."

Who will you help DREAM BIG?

POCAHONTAS

Pocahontas is part of the Powhatan tribe and daughter of the chief. She is a noble, free-spirited, and highly spiritual young woman, lovingly nicknamed "Little Mischief" by her father. She expresses wisdom beyond her years and offers kindness and guidance to those around her. She loves her homeland, adventure, and nature.

THREE SISTERS

WRITTEN BY ELIZABETH RUDNICK & ILLUSTRATED BY ALICE X. ZHANG AND STUDIO IBOIX
SPECIAL THANKS TO CULTURAL CONSULTANT DAWN JACKSON (SAGINAW CHIPPEWA)

The air was crisp and cool as Pocahontas walked through the woods. Beneath her feet, leaves the color of a warm fire crunched and made the air sing. Pocahontas smiled. Fall had arrived. It was Pocahontas's favorite time of year. Change was everywhere. And with that change came the promise of new adventures.

"Isn't it just beautiful, Meeko?" she said, turning to look at the gray-and-black raccoon scampering by her side. The little creature looked up and chattered in answer. She laughed. Meeko didn't love fall—or the winter that would follow. To him, it meant cold nights, short days, and less food. But Pocahontas wasn't worried. She and her people had been working and living on this land for generations. They knew the best way to make it through the hard winter.

Pushing past some low branches, Pocahontas entered the outskirts of her village. It was busy. Most of the men were off hunting or fishing in order to stock up for the coming months. A few of the younger men had stayed behind to protect the village. Nodding at one of them now, Pocahontas called out a greeting. The young man tried to keep his face serious, but as Pocahontas passed, he broke out in a wide smile.

Moving farther into the village, Pocahontas and Meeko arrived in front of what would be a new *yi-hakan*. The frame of the longhouse was starting to take shape. Conversations flowed between the

POCAHONTAS IS . . .

BOLD
A PROTECTOR
DARING
RESPECTFUL OF NATURE
GENEROUS
SPIRITUAL

POCAHONTAS'S DREAM:

To have the courage to walk in another's footsteps

HEROIC MOMENT:

A cry for peace to stop a war between settlers and her tribe

SIDEKICKS:

Meeko and Flit

FAMOUS QUOTE:

"My dream is pointing me down another path."

friends, sisters, mothers, and daughters as they completed the various tasks that were required to build the longhouse. It was the job of the women of her tribe to build the homes, and they took great pride in their work.

Pocahontas watched for a moment. She had built many homes with these same women, but it still amazed her. Building a home from the nature around them was a part of their tradition and culture. And over the years, the process did not change. Some women worked the saplings, bending them until they created a *U* shape. Others were sewing the mats that would eventually become the roof. Still others were collecting wood that would be used to fuel the fire and keep the home warm through the long winter. And still others worked with furs to create warm blankets that would end up on the floor or low benches that lined the yi-hakan.

Spotting her friend Nakoma struggling with a long sapling branch, Pocahontas rushed over to help. "Here," she said, pushing down on the branch. The wood bent beneath the pressure of their hands until both ends touched the ground. A half a dozen more had already been shaped and placed in the ground. Eventually, they would form a long, low building that looked like the tunnels gophers created underground.

"Thanks, Pocahontas," Nakoma said, standing up and brushing a strand of dark hair from her face. "I was having trouble with that one. The wood might not be ready. But we don't have time to wait. The family must move in soon." Behind them, the sun was already dipping toward the horizon, making the air chilly.

Pocahontas nodded. She knew that the young couple who had recently married would want to move into their new home before the first frost. So it was up to all of them to get the house ready. Fast. "I'll come back to help soon," she said to Nakoma. "I just need to go check on my crops."

Nakoma smiled. "Of course," she said. "We will be here. And we will have need of your Three Sisters," she added, referring to the corn, beans, and squash that Pocahontas had planted in the spring. Nakoma raised her eyes to the cloudless, sunny sky. "I have a feeling it will be a long winter this year."

Pocahontas followed her friend's gaze. In the air above, a flock of geese flew south, the *V*-shaped flight pattern and trumpeting calls heralding the cooler weather to come. It was hard to imagine a time when the same sky would be steel gray and the ground covered in snow. But the seasons' changes were as inevitable as the geese's migration.

Saying another farewell, Pocahontas moved beyond the last of the village houses to where plots of land had been dug up and planted. Kneeling down, Pocahontas felt the warm dirt on her knees and took a deep breath. The Three Sisters were thriving and almost ready to be harvested. She eyed the bright colors of her garden. The green shades of the corn and beans; the orange and yellow hues of the squash. The colors burst, alive and vibrant with the promise of the sustenance they would provide. Kneeling down, she ran her fingers along a smooth stalk of corn, trailing them through the silky threads at the top of the cob before squeezing a plump bean. Pocahontas smiled, pleased with her work.

Hearing voices, Pocahontas rose to her feet and turned. A village guard was approaching. Behind him were three Englishwomen. Pocahontas brightened when she saw that one of them was her friend, Purity Williams. Purity's eyes were bright with excitement as she looked around. The other two young women did not look as pleased. These were Purity's sisters—Patience and Prudence. While Purity's energy glimmered like the autumn leaves in the sun, Patience's and Prudence's demeanors were dull and lifeless. Clearly, they were not happy to be here.

"Purity!" Pocahontas said, eagerly walking over. When she saw the worry on the young guard's face, she gave him a reassuring smile. She did not blame him for his concern. It had not been all that long ago that the English had arrived and tensions had arisen between the two groups. But under Pocahontas's urging and example, her tribe had made peace with the English. While a few had returned to England, those who stayed had remained amicable and respectful of the peace forged by Pocahontas along with her father,

Chief Powhatan, and the Englishman John Smith. Still, the guard was young and it was not surprising he would feel a twinge of fear at the arrival of English in the village. Everyone was still learning this new way of life. "Don't worry. These ladies are my friends. They are not a threat."

Nodding, the young man stepped back and slipped away.

"Hello, Pocahontas," Purity said, walking up to her. Pocahontas returned the young woman's warm smile. She and Purity had only just become friends, but Pocahontas found the bright and lively young woman to be great company. She had visited her in the English village several times, but this was the first time Purity had come to her. "I was hoping you might show us your village," she said now. "My sisters were so excited when I mentioned we might come." She looked over at Prudence and Patience. The girls didn't say anything. Patience simply shrugged and Prudence's frown only deepened.

Pocahontas bit back a laugh. She was quite sure that Purity's sisters had had no desire to come. But Purity was persuasive when she wanted to be. She should have been named Perseverance. "Of course," Pocahontas said. "I would be happy to show you all around."

"Wonderful," Purity said, clasping her hands together in glee. She pointed to the plants growing in front of them. "Are you harvesting this food? Now?"

Pocahontas nodded. "I will shortly," she replied. "We plant these in the spring and then wait until the first frost before we harvest the crops. That allows them to grow longer." One by one, she showed the three sisters her own Three Sisters—the corn, beans, and squash. "It is important that we plant these three crops with one another. Alone, they would do okay, but they are stronger, and grow better, when planted together. These will keep us fed through the winter."

To her surprise, Patience let out a laugh. But it wasn't a kind laugh. "*You* do the planting?" she asked. "Why?"

"Yes, why?" added Prudence, her heavy brows drawing even closer together.

Pocahontas was silent for a moment. She understood that the Englishwomen led very different lives than her people did. Taking a breath, Pocahontas explained. "It is the women's job in our village to harvest the crops. We must make sure that we have enough food for everyone, not just our own family, when winter arrives. The more food we grow, the more we harvest, the better we will eat."

"But *you* do all that work?" Prudence said. "That is just the silliest thing I've ever heard. Don't the men go out to gather food come winter? That is what our men do when we need food or provisions. It is, after all, the job of the men to provide food for us. Not the other way around. Then we prepare it."

"Prudence!" Purity said in a harsh tone. "Not every culture is the same." Turning to her friend, she shrugged. "Pardon my sister. She does not always think before she speaks. *I* think it is wonderful that you have such an important job."

A loud shout from back in the village startled the group. Prudence and Patience took a step back, a flash of fear crossing their faces. But Pocahontas was not concerned, just curious. Moving past the two women, she headed toward the sound.

"I'm so sorry," Purity said in a whisper, falling into step beside her. Behind them, Prudence and Patience reluctantly followed. "I thought this would be fun for my sisters. They just sit about the house all day complaining. I thought a walk might do them some good."

"Don't be sorry," Pocahontas said, reaching over and giving her friend's arm a squeeze. "I'm glad to see a friend. Is all well with you?"

A flash of sadness crossed over her friend's usually cheerful face. "It is fine," she said, still whispering. "I just worry that we are not ready for the winter ahead. Not like you are."

The young woman had reason to worry. Pocahontas had seen the English settlement, and it was still a long way from ready for winter. But she did not say that aloud. She knew it would only make Purity worry more. Instead, Pocahontas slowed her pace so that the sisters could catch up with them. They were holding the long skirts of their dresses up as they daintily tiptoed their way over the ground.

"Do you not have stones or a path to walk on?" Prudence whined.

"Quite right," Patience added in her own whiny voice.

Purity leaned in to whisper to Pocahontas, "We don't have nice footpaths either. My sisters still think this new land should look like a bustling English city."

"And what is that smell?" Patience crinkled her nose. "It smells like wet wood."

"It is," Pocahontas replied. "We have collected wood to dry out. Wet wood does not burn as well and will make our homes smoky. So we dry the wood now so that it will be ready to use when the days grow colder."

Prudence shivered. "Colder?" she repeated. "It feels quite chilly already. I should have worn my shawl, but Purity was in such a rush I left it at home. I'm practically freezing."

"I'm sorry to hear that," Pocahontas said. Spotting a fur blanket lying on a low bench outside one of the homes, she offered it to Prudence.

The young woman recoiled as if the fur might suddenly become the living animal it had once belonged to. "I would rather shiver," she said.

Pocahontas shrugged. She had tried.

Continuing, they finally arrived at the source of the shout. It was the work site for the new home. Purity's eyes lit up when she saw the structure. "Oh my!" she said. "Look at that! It's like a skeleton of a house!"

Pocahontas let out a laugh. "Yes," she said. "It is not nearly done, but we are working hard."

"You?" Patience said. "Don't tell me you build homes as well as harvest your own crops." She shook her head. "You certainly are a strange group."

Pocahontas cocked her head. "Strange?" she repeated. "This is not strange. This is our tradition. We build our homes. Why would we not? We own them, after all."

To her shock, both Patience and Prudence looked horrified. "What do you mean you own them? Surely you mean your husbands own them," Patience said, speaking for both her and Prudence.

Purity shot her sister a look before turning back to the work site. "I think this is remarkable," she said. "We are given no say in our homes, except in how to decorate them. And what is that over there?" she asked, pointing to a round hole in the middle of the structure.

"That will be the fire pit," Pocahontas explained. "For the wood we collect. There will be sleeping mats nearby, and we can cook over the fire as well. We dry some of the meat the men have hunted during the summer months and add it to our vegetables. Some of it we smoke to eat on its own." She remembered what Prudence had said about their men hunting. "It is hard to find animals in the winter. Like us, they hunker down to stay warm. Some even sleep the entire winter. Though we don't have that luxury." Pocahontas said the last part with a smile, hoping to bring one to the faces of Prudence and Patience.

But Prudence just scowled. "Well, I think we've seen enough, Purity," she said. "I would like to return home now—where we do things a woman *should* do. Not play at house building and harvesting." Turning on her heel, she started off. But her steps were slowed by her long dress and she ended up waddling more than storming off. Patience walked off after her.

With an apologetic glance at Pocahontas, Purity turned to follow her sisters. "Thank you," she said over her shoulder. "I loved seeing all of this. I hope I can come again soon—perhaps alone next time." And with a small smile, she, too, left.

Watching them go, Pocahontas frowned. She knew that this was a new world for the Englishwomen. She just wished that they would be a bit more open to the differences.

A few weeks later, Pocahontas stood in front of the completed longhouse. She smiled as she saw the women of the village gathered around, helping the new couple fill the home with furs and mats. It had been hard work, but they had finished the home and gathered the crops—and just in time, it would seem. Looking up, she saw the clouds were heavy and gray. A storm was coming.

As if sensing her thoughts, a single flake of snow drifted down from the sky. A moment later another fell, and then another and another. Almost instantly, the sky was filled with white. This wasn't just a storm; this was the worst kind of storm—an early winter squall. Anyone caught outside or unaware would be in danger of frostbite, or worse.

Following others, Pocahontas made her way into her own longhouse. Settling in beside the warm fire, Pocahontas listened as her father and several other elders of the tribe spoke of what the early storm could mean. She heard "English," "sign," and "danger" among other things and let out a sad sigh. She had hoped that this winter would be an easy one for all of them. Adjusting to the arrival of the English was difficult enough. Adding a long season of storms might only serve to heighten any underlying tensions.

The storm raged outside, but inside her longhouse, Pocahontas felt safe and warm. They were prepared, even for this early storm. And while she knew it would mean more work when the storm was over, Pocahontas secretly liked the weather. It brought people together, and despite the dangers outside, Pocahontas heard the warm rumble of good conversation from inside the longhouse and from the longhouses all around.

She was just settling in to work on a mat as a gift for the new family when the flap of her own home burst inward, bringing with it a scattering of snow. One of the young men from her tribe stood in the entry, his dark hair covered in white. There was a shape behind him, and as he stepped farther inside, the shape took form, revealing Purity.

Pocahontas leaped to her feet and rushed to her friend. Purity was shivering beneath a cloak, her fair cheeks red with cold. "Pocahontas!" she cried. "You must help us! The roof on our house wasn't ready for this storm. It completely collapsed, and my family is freezing." She nodded over her shoulder. "They are here with me, if that is okay?"

"I just need to ask my father," Pocahontas said. Turning, she made her way to where her father sat. His face was stern, as if he already knew the question she was going to ask. She quickly told him what had happened. For a moment, Chief Powhatan hesitated. Pocahontas held her breath. She knew she was asking a lot. To share their food and fire would drain their own resources. But her father had taught her to value right and wrong. And turning their back on Purity's family now would be wrong. Finally, he nodded.

Giving her father a quick hug, Pocahontas turned back and made her way to Purity. "Your family is welcome in our home until the storm passes," she said.

"Oh, thank you, Pocahontas!" Purity said, grabbing her hands and squeezing them tightly. "Thank you." After ducking back outside, she returned a moment later with Patience, Prudence, and an older couple who, based on the dour expressions just like Patience's and Prudence's, must have been their parents.

"Welcome," Pocahontas said. "Please, warm yourself by the fire. And I will get you some food. You must be hungry."

Patience, the ever-present scowl on her face, nodded. "We will not trouble you for long. We can see how cramped you are already." She gestured at the various villagers who had gathered in the longhouse of the chief.

"Patience! Enough!" Purity said, her expression stern. "You will be grateful for the hospitality Pocahontas and her family are showing us. Now sit down. And be quiet."

Pocahontas smiled proudly. Purity was a force stronger than any storm. She watched as her friend's family slowly made their way inside and closer to the fire. At first, the villagers were quiet, waiting to see what would happen next. But as the minutes ticked by, the longhouse grew warmer—both in temperature and mood.

Sitting beside Purity, Pocahontas laughed as several of the younger children of the village tried to play with Patience and Prudence. "I don't think they realize my sisters have never had fun—even when they were kids themselves," Purity whispered.

"Just watch," Pocahontas whispered back. "I bet they will have them playing along soon enough."

As the storm continued to blow outside, Pocahontas and several of the other women brought out food from their stores. They passed it along, and because of the good harvest, no one went without.

"This is delicious," Purity's mother exclaimed after her first bite of the stewed corn and squash. "We must be sure to get the recipe from you, Pocahontas."

"I do not believe we have recipes like you are used to, Mistress Williams," Pocahontas said kindly. "But I would be happy to show you how we make it sometime, if you would like."

"Please," Mistress Williams said. "You are welcome in our home at any time. After all, you have so graciously opened yours."

Nodding, Pocahontas turned to her own plate. But, feeling eyes on her, she looked up. Prudence and Patience were standing in front of her. To her surprise, they both looked rather . . . sheepish. "We just wanted to say—" Prudence started.

"—that we're sorry for how rude we were—" Patience added.

"—the other week," Prudence finished. "We were wrong to judge you. Purity was right. You are strong and have so much knowledge about this place. We don't understand it all. Not yet." She paused and listened as the wind howled outside. "I wonder if, uh . . ."

"I think what she means to say," Purity said, joining her sisters, "is that perhaps you might be so kind as to teach us a bit. For next winter, that is. How to grow crops, maybe?" She looked at the plates of food, full despite the storm raging outside.

Prudence nodded. A small smile formed on her face. It made Prudence look years younger, and Pocahontas finally saw a bit of family resemblance to Purity. "Yes, perhaps, come spring, you might be willing to show us how to plant as well. The—what did you call them?"

"Three Sisters," Pocahontas answered. "Yes, of course. And until then, we will share our food and our fire." She paused and looked around the longhouse, full of people so different but brought together by the same needs. Change had certainly come to their village with the shift of the season. But it was a change for good. "Like the Three Sisters," Pocahontas added,

"we are—and always will be—STRONGER when we GROW together."

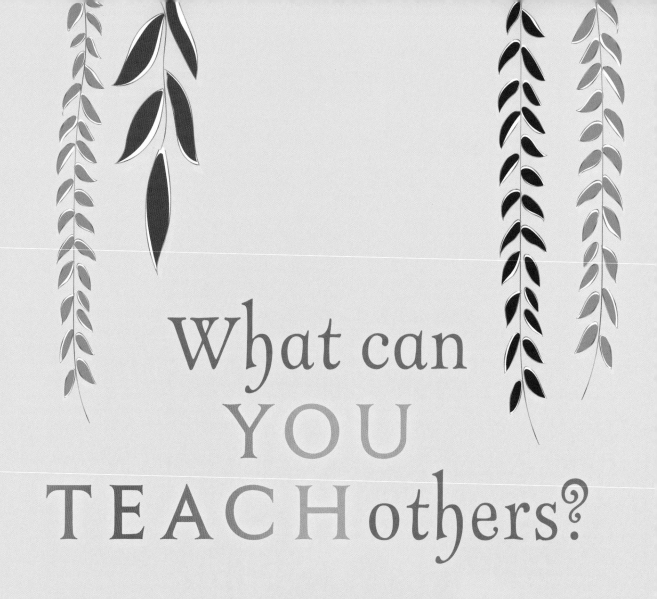

What can YOU TEACH others?

JASMINE

Jasmine is the princess of Agrabah. She is incredibly independent and strong. She isn't afraid to speak her mind no matter who she's up against, and she'll never hesitate to stand up for what's right, especially for someone else's sake. She is extremely compassionate and caring toward her kingdom, her family, and her friends.

THE PRINCESS POLO GAMES

WRITTEN BY KITTY RICHARDS & ILLUSTRATED BY NABI H. ALI

One morning during breakfast, Jasmine received a letter from the Princess Polo Club.

"It's finally here!" Jasmine exclaimed.

Jasmine's father, the Sultan, looked on excitedly while Rajah, her loyal tiger, nosed the tray holding the letter. Aladdin and his monkey, Abu, craned their necks expectantly. Even the Genie fell silent as he waited for Jasmine to share her news. She tore open the envelope and read:

Dear Princess Jasmine,
Congratulations! You have been selected
to be a Princess Polo Club team captain.
Please report to Qamar Field tomorrow morning
to meet your team: the Royal Raiders.
Thank you,
The Princess Polo Club

Jasmine explained that the Princess Polo Games only happened once a year. Princesses from kingdoms far and wide came to compete. This year, the games were being held in Agrabah, and Jasmine wanted nothing more than to win the Princess Polo Club's golden trophy, just as her mother had many years earlier.

"How exciting!" Aladdin said. Abu chattered in agreement.

The Genie nodded. "I can't wait to cheer you on!" With a poof of blue sparks, he transformed into a cheerleader complete with a megaphone and pom-poms. "Go, Jasmine!"

The Sultan beamed in delight. "I wish your mother were here to see you following in her footsteps," he told his daughter.

"Me too," Jasmine replied. Polo was a game Jasmine had loved since she was a young girl. She loved playing in the open air, feeling the strength of her horse as it galloped down the field, and that magical feeling of connection with her teammates. But most of all, she loved that polo was something that connected her to her mother, who had loved the sport and had given Jasmine her first mallet.

Excusing herself from the breakfast table, Jasmine held tightly to the letter and made her way to a corridor she loved to visit. The soft patter of her feet was the only sound in the grand marble hallway. Jasmine came to a stop in front of a giant tapestry on the wall. On it was a woven image of her mother's polo team. The four teammates gleefully celebrated as they stood on the winning pedestal. Jasmine's mother stood front and center, proudly holding a golden trophy.

"I will do my best to win the trophy, Mama," Jasmine whispered. "I'll win it for you."

The next morning, warm sunlight burst over the kingdom of Agrabah. Jasmine quickly readied herself for the day ahead, stopping to see if the Magic Carpet would fly with her to the field. With a swirl in the air and a shake of its tassels, the carpet was ready!

"Bye, Father! See you soon, everybody!" Jasmine called as she jumped on the carpet. "Wish me luck!"

The duo flew off the balcony and away from the palace grounds over to Qamar Field. Jasmine's stomach fluttered like a flock of doves.

She stepped onto the field and stood next to three other young women. They all introduced themselves. Then an older woman approached, her stride graceful and strong, and stood before them. Jasmine thought the woman looked familiar, but she couldn't quite place her face.

"Welcome, captains!" the woman said. "I am the chairwoman of the Princess Polo Club. In a moment, I will introduce you to your teams. It is up to you to train them well. At the end of our season, a final match will determine who wins the golden trophy."

"That will be me," one young woman replied confidently. "I'm Princess Farah. I always win, no matter what."

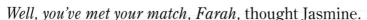

Well, you've met your match, Farah, thought Jasmine.

The chairwoman announced each team. First, there were the Majestic Monarchs. Three princesses in matching magenta outfits came riding out, sitting tall in their saddles. The Super Sultanas came out next. They were equally impressive, dressed in green. As were the Awesome Aces, who wore orange uniforms and had a fierce look in their eyes.

Jasmine's heart thrummed with excitement. Her team was next. She couldn't wait to meet the women she would lead to victory!

"And last but not least," the chairwoman announced, "Princesses Kamali, Amira, and Zayna: the Royal Raiders!"

Jasmine beamed, but then her smile faltered as her teammates appeared.

Princess Farah sniffed. "More like the Royal *Afraiders*."

The three princesses on Jasmine's team didn't so much ride onto the field as wander out as if they had no clue where they were going. Princess Kamali was holding on to her horse's neck for dear life, clearly terrified she would fall off. Princess Amira had her nose buried in a book, paying no attention as her horse steered itself toward a particularly succulent patch of grass and started munching. And Princess Zayna had hopped off her horse and was doing handstands and cartwheels across the field.

As Farah snickered, Jasmine squared her shoulders. She wasn't ready to give up on her teammates. She would do whatever it took to get them competition ready.

The teams dispersed across the field to begin practice, and Jasmine handed out mallets to her teammates. But Kamali would barely let go of her horse's neck long enough to grab her mallet.

Amira tucked hers under her elbow as she eagerly turned a page in her book. Meanwhile, Zayna twirled her mallet around like a baton.

Jasmine bit her lip and decided the best way to coach her team into shape would be to give them some tough love.

She cleared her throat and barked out orders. "Kamali, sit up straight! There's nothing to be afraid of." She turned toward the other teammates. "Put away the book, Amira. Do you think you're in the library? And, Zayna, get back on your saddle, now!"

The princesses stared at her. Then Zayna burst into tears mid-handstand.

Before Jasmine had a chance to change her approach, the horse Amira was absentmindedly riding bumped into Kamali's horse, spooking it. The horse reared up! If Kamali was scared before, she was even more so now. The horse took off running with Kamali clinging to its mane. They headed straight for Zayna, who was still in the middle of a handstand. Zayna jumped out of the way just in time, her tears momentarily forgotten.

Jasmine couldn't believe her eyes; nothing was going as planned. Her team didn't even know how to hold their mallets! Worse, they didn't seem to have any interest whatsoever in winning the competition. Jasmine's hopes for the golden trophy were fading.

"Practice is over," Jasmine said with a sigh. "Come back tomorrow, ready to play."

With her spirits low, Jasmine went to speak with the chairwoman, who was sitting in the bleachers. "There has to be some mistake," Jasmine pleaded. "My teammates have no idea what they're doing!"

The chairwoman shook her head and smiled warmly. "Teams

were chosen specifically for each captain's strengths. You can do this, Princess Jasmine."

When Jasmine returned home, the Genie tried to cheer her up. He stretched his bright blue face into the shape of a horse's. "Why the long face?" he asked.

But Jasmine didn't even smile.

"How did your first practice go?" asked Aladdin that night.

"Not very well," she said. "I'm never going to win that trophy."

"Just do your best," said Aladdin. Jasmine hoped her best would be good enough.

The next day, Jasmine came to the field armed with patience. She invited her teammates to tie up their horses and sit next to her in the grass.

"I think we need to START FRESH!"

she said. "Polo is a game, and games are fun. Let's begin by learning the basics. Like how to sit on a horse, how to hold a mallet, and how to hit a ball. Does that sound like a good plan?"

The princesses looked at each other and then nodded at Jasmine.

"Great," Jasmine said, smiling brightly. "Let's get started."

Step by step, she taught her team how to play polo. She showed them how to hit the ball into the goal and how to stop the opposing team from bumping their horses or hooking their mallets. Soon Kamali, Amira, and Zayna were starting to get the hang of the game. There were still some mishaps—like when Zayna tried to leap from her horse onto Kamali's, or when Amira's horse started eating pages of her book. But this time, the team dissolved into giggles instead of tears.

With each practice, Jasmine's team got better at playing polo—and Jasmine became an even better team captain. She had initially thought that being a team captain meant telling her teammates what to do. But she had learned that it worked better to be supportive and find ways to boost each teammate's confidence.

As the tournament grew closer, Jasmine knew her team was ready to try a new type of practice. "Today we'll play a *different* game!" Jasmine told the princesses. She set up a zigzag pattern of balls around the field. "Let's see who can hit the most balls!"

Kamali, Amira, and Zayna raced down the field. Jasmine saw that Kamali was so determined to stay on her horse that she would bump into the other players to stop them from bumping into her!

Amira turned out to be an amazing hitter—as long as she pretended she was a hero from one of her books.

And once Zayna realized her horse was as energetic as she was, they made a great team. They always got to the ball first!

"Hey, look at me!" Kamali called out. "I'm playing polo!"

"Me too!" cried Amira.

"Me three!" shouted Zayna.

Jasmine couldn't help smiling. Her team might not have the most talent, but they were learning the rules. And best of all, they were having fun doing it.

At last the tournament arrived and the real playing began. Some matches they won and some they lost. But each game, Jasmine encouraged her teammates to use their strengths to do their best. Soon they won enough games to earn a place in the finals against the Majestic Monarchs!

"Great job, team," Jasmine said as the princesses steered their horses to the stable, proudly caressing their manes. "Let's head home for some rest. Tomorrow is the big game!"

As everyone headed off the field, Jasmine fell into step behind her team and some players from the Majestic Monarchs, who had finished their game at the same time as the Royal Raiders.

"Today's games were fun, but I sure am exhausted," said Amira, yawning.

"At least you can enjoy your win," said a Monarchs player. "Farah is so mean. She's always yelling at us to ride faster and play harder. Nothing we do is ever good enough."

Another Monarch player joined in. "Maybe Farah needs to borrow your book, Amira," she said, nodding at the book's title: *How to Win as a Team*. "Our team captain doesn't know the definition of *team*. I just want to get tomorrow's game over with."

Jasmine listened, her eyes wide. She wished she could do something to make sure everyone enjoyed playing polo.

That night before bed, Jasmine gazed at her mother's polo

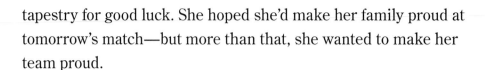

tapestry for good luck. She hoped she'd make her family proud at tomorrow's match—but more than that, she wanted to make her team proud.

The next day, the city of Agrabah seemed to buzz with excitement. When Jasmine arrived at the field, she saw that the stands were filled with family and friends. Jasmine could see her own family huddled together and already cheering. The Sultan was sitting atop Rajah to get a better view, clapping as each horse and player strode onto the field. The Genie had multiplied himself into a full marching band complete with outfits and instruments. And Aladdin and Abu were cheering so loudly that Jasmine could hear them from across the field!

Just as Jasmine was rounding up her team for a quick pep talk, Princess Farah crossed their path on her horse.

"Well, if it isn't the scaredy-cat, the bookworm, and the jumping bean," said Farah. "Get ready to lose!" she shouted as her horse galloped down the field.

Jasmine's cheeks grew warm with anger, but she shrugged off the feeling to focus on her team. They huddled together moments before the first chukker, or game period. "Farah doesn't know that the very things she teases you for are the things that make you special," Jasmine said.

"I never realized how much I'd love riding," Kamali said, giving her horse a fond scratch between the ears. "I can't wait to block Farah from scoring!"

Amira grinned. "And I love imagining I'm an Egyptian charioteer while I play. Maybe I'll score my first goal today!"

"And there's nothing I love more than zooming across the field," said Zayna, her eyes sparkling. "Oh, I hope we win the tournament."

Jasmine smiled. "Me too. Now let's get out there and have fun!"

The game began. Zayna beat Farah to the ball right away, earning the Royal Raiders the first possession.

In the second chukker, Kamali stopped Farah from scoring not once, not twice, but three times!

Amira scored two goals all by herself in the third chukker. One of them was from all the way across the field!

Then the ball headed right for Farah and Jasmine. They raced after it. Jasmine rode alongside Farah and expertly bumped her out of the way. Jasmine headed for the goal, ready to score. But then she saw Zayna. Jasmine hit the ball to her. Zayna's face lit up and she aimed, shot, and connected with a resounding *THWACK!* Jasmine watched in delight as the ball bounced toward the goal . . . but Farah intercepted it.

The Majestic Monarchs were in perfect position to make a goal. Farah's teammates called out for her to pass the ball. But she ignored them, raced down the field, and scored a goal on her own. Farah held her mallet up in the air victoriously. "That's how you do it!" she shouted to her teammates.

"Ball hog," one of the Monarchs muttered.

After the fourth chukker, the captains rallied their teams.

"Great job, Royal Raiders!" exclaimed Jasmine.

"The score is tied," said Amira. "We could actually win this!"

The other Royal Raiders squealed with excitement. But when Jasmine peeked over her team's huddle at the Majestic Monarchs, she could see their shoulders droop as Farah gestured wildly at the goal. Jasmine had noticed that Farah never passed the ball to her teammates, and she felt sad for them. That gave her an idea.

She turned her attention back to the team. "Team, I'm so proud of you," Jasmine said. "Amira, you made not only your first goal, but a second, too! Zayna, you raced to the ball from the get-go and got us the first possession. And, Kamali, I've never seen anyone block the other team from scoring so many times!" She paused and took a deep breath. "But I'm not sure the other team is having as much fun as we are."

Jasmine huddled her team close and told them her idea. She wanted to give the other team a chance to play and have fun. The other women agreed at once!

When the Royal Raiders returned to the field for the final chukker, Jasmine got the first possession. She could have raced down the field to score the winning goal, but she passed the ball—not to her team, but straight to one of the Monarchs players! Kamali and Amira, in on the plan, blocked Farah from intercepting the pass, and Zayna cheered the Monarchs all the way down the field.

In the last chukker, each Monarchs player scored a goal! When the final bell rang, the Monarchs had won.

Even though she'd lost the tournament, Jasmine's heart was full. It was a tough game, but most important, it was fun. She was pleased that everyone on both teams had gotten a chance to play and let their talents shine. That was more important than winning.

At the awards ceremony, Farah and her team stepped up to the podium.

"Congratulations," said the chairwoman. "The medals go to the winners: the Majestic Monarchs!" She stepped forward and hung medals around each of their necks.

Jasmine and her team cheered along with the rest of the crowd. Farah grinned as she looked down at her medal, but her smile faded when the chairwoman held tight to the golden trophy.

Just as Jasmine and her team were preparing to head off the field, the chairwoman spoke again. "There is one more award to be given out today," she said, holding up the trophy. "This year, the golden trophy goes to . . . Princess Jasmine!"

"I . . . I don't understand," Jasmine stammered.

"It is Princess Polo Club tradition to bestow the golden trophy on the most honorable player, not the winning team," explained the chairwoman. "Jasmine, you showed strength, bravery, and most of all, kindness to your teammates *and* opponents. You are a true leader—just like your mother."

Jasmine gasped. "You knew my mother?"

The chairwoman nodded. "She was *my* team captain."

No wonder she looked familiar. She was one of the women from her mother's tapestry!

Jasmine's heart soared and the crowd roared with applause. Her family hurried out of the stands to congratulate her.

"You were amazing out there," said Aladdin, smiling proudly.

Rajah rubbed against her legs, and Abu wrapped his arms around the gleaming trophy.

The Genie turned himself into a rocket and blasted off, bursting overhead into a colorful fireworks display.

"Like mother, like daughter," the chairwoman said to Jasmine's father.

"I told you so," he said, embracing his daughter. "And I've never been prouder."

What is your
your
PROUDEST
WIN?

AURORA

When Princess Aurora was born, the evil fairy Maleficent placed a curse on her. To protect the young princess, King Stefan and the Queen sent her to the forest to be raised by the three good fairies, Flora, Fauna, and Merryweather. After Aurora and Prince Phillip broke the curse by defeating Maleficent, they went to live at the castle. But Aurora still calls the fairies' cottage her second home and visits often.

THE MISSING WANDS

WRITTEN BY ERIN FALLIGANT & ILLUSTRATED BY LIAM BRAZIER

"Hello?" Princess Aurora knocked sharply on the door of the thatched-roof cottage. She had traveled all the way from the castle to visit the three good fairies, but she'd been knocking for several minutes. Were they even home?

The front door suddenly flew open. As Flora burst out, her red hat slipped sideways over her gray curls. "Thank goodness you're here!" she cried.

Aurora placed a comforting hand on the fairy's shoulder. "Flora, what's wrong? Has something happened?"

Merryweather pushed past Flora. "Someone has stolen our wands," she announced, her round face flushed with anger. "When we find them, I'll turn that thief into a warty old toad!"

"Now, now, Merryweather," said Fauna, following close behind. "I'm sure the wands weren't stolen." But her brow was wrinkled with worry.

Flora paced the cobblestone walk. "We've looked everywhere! Whatever will we do without our magic?"

Merryweather sucked in her breath. "How will we protect ourselves from evil?"

"Or spread happiness?" asked Fauna.

"How will we fly?" said Merryweather, throwing her arms wide. "Or clean? Or even cook?"

197

AURORA IS . . .

LOVING
JOYFUL
GOOD-NATURED
FRIENDLY
GRACEFUL
IMAGINATIVE
HOPEFUL

AURORA'S DREAM:

To be free to explore life's
possibilities

HEROIC MOMENT:

Never giving up on her belief
that dreams really do come true

SIDEKICKS:

Flora, Fauna, and Merryweather

FAMOUS QUOTE:

"If you dream a thing more than
once, it's sure to come true."

Fauna's face lit up. "Maybe
I could do the cooking," she
suggested.

Merryweather sighed. "I think
I just lost my appetite."

"Don't worry," said Aurora,
gathering the fairies around her.
"I'll help you look for your wands,
and we won't need magic to find
them. You lived for many years
without your magic, when you
were keeping me safe from . . ."

Maleficent. Aurora could
scarcely say the name of the evil
fairy who had placed a curse on
her long before. To protect Aurora,
the good fairies had hidden her
in that very cottage and raised
her for sixteen years. During
that time, they had vowed not to
use their magic, to avoid calling
attention to their whereabouts.

Fauna's brown eyes grew
misty. "I remember, dear. Those
were happy times."

"They were," said Aurora,
her heart squeezing. "We did all

sorts of things without magic, didn't we? So I know that if we all work together now, we can find your wands."

Flora was already working on a plan. "We need to retrace our steps!" she announced. "When did we last use our wands?"

Fauna's face brightened. "I used mine to make a cup of tea after our picnic, remember?"

"Yes, and I used mine to fold up the picnic blanket," said Merryweather. "We were sitting in our favorite spot by the stream!" She hurried toward the woods, gathering her blue skirt as she ran.

Aurora linked arms with Flora. "Good thinking," she said to her fairy friend.

When they reached the stream, Merryweather and Fauna were already searching the grassy banks. "Hmm . . . we sat right about here, didn't we?" said Merryweather.

Aurora dropped to her knees to help them look. Just then, a squirrel darted past, dragging a long narrow twig. But when Aurora glanced up, she saw that it wasn't a twig at all. She gasped and pointed. "Look!"

"My wand!" cried Merryweather. "Stop, thief!" She chased the squirrel toward the stream.

When the squirrel leaped off the grassy bank, Merryweather did, too. When the squirrel jumped onto a flat stone in the middle of the stream, Merryweather did, too. But as the squirrel sprang to the other side, it dropped the wand. Merryweather lunged for it and . . .

Plunk! Splash! She tumbled into the cool water.

When the fairy stood up, she was dripping wet. "Where's my wand?" she cried, spinning in a circle. "There!"

The wand was floating downstream, caught up in the current. As Merryweather splashed after it, Aurora raced along the bank. Aurora jumped into the ankle-deep water, reaching for the wand as it sailed past. But the current was too fast! The wand bobbed around a bend and then another before disappearing. Aurora helped a soaking Merryweather onto the riverbank before stepping out of the stream herself.

Merryweather sputtered as she wrung out her wet cape. "That b-bothersome squirrel! Why, I ought to . . ."

"Now, now," said Aurora, "I'm sure the squirrel had a perfectly good reason for taking your wand."

"Yes," said Fauna. "Maybe the squirrel needed your wand for something."

"Perhaps to build a nest?" suggested Flora, peering up at the branches of a nearby tree.

Aurora followed her gaze and spotted some twigs sticking out of a hole in the tree. "There it is!" she said. "Well done, Flora. I'll bet your wands are in that nest."

Merryweather hurried toward the tree, stepped on a nearby stump, and slid off her hat before sticking her head into the tree hollow. "Good news, Fauna," she called in a muffled voice. "I see your wand!"

"Do you really?" Fauna asked. "Oh, let me see!"

She scrambled onto the stump next to Merryweather, but there was only enough room for each fairy to balance on one foot.

Fauna looked into the tree hollow. "That's it!" she said, reaching inside.

Just then, the squirrel scrambled down the tree trunk. It perched on a branch above Fauna and Merryweather and chattered as if scolding them.

"Fauna," Merryweather whispered, nudging the other fairy, "hurry up."

"I almost have it," Fauna said. "Just a little farther—"

The squirrel continued its angry chattering, scampering closer until it was nearly nose to nose with Merryweather.

"Oh!" Merryweather cried. As she leaned back, her heel began to slip off of the stump.

"I've got it!" Fauna declared, pulling her wand out of the hole.

At the very same moment, Merryweather flailed, losing her balance, and grabbed on to Fauna's cape as she fell.

Thud! The two fairies landed in a heap.

"Oh, dear," Fauna said. She held up her wand, which was bent in two places. When she tried to cast a spell to fix it, the wand sputtered and smoked.

"I'm sorry, Fauna," Aurora said, her heart sinking.

The squirrel chattered once more at the fairies and sat in front of the tree hollow as if to block them from reentering.

Merryweather huffed. "I don't understand why that squirrel got so upset."

"Perhaps we shouldn't have touched its nest," Fauna said with a sigh. She tried to straighten out her wand, but it was no use.

"Fauna is right," said Aurora softly. "We wouldn't want someone rattling around in our homes, would we?"

Flora shook her head. "No, I suppose we wouldn't."

Aurora helped the fairies to their feet and picked a few leaves and sticks out of Fauna's hair. But as she untangled the last twig, she realized it was no twig at all—it was the third wand!

"It must have gotten stuck in Fauna's hair while she was trying to pull her own wand from the nest!" Aurora said, extending the wand to Flora.

Before Flora could take it, the squirrel raced down the trunk of the tree, snatched the wand, and leaped to the forest floor. Then it disappeared into a thicket.

"Follow that squirrel!" ordered Merryweather. She charged through the bushes.

"Don't scare it away!" cried Fauna, following close behind.

Aurora and the fairies raced after the squirrel. But the bushes were dense, and the squirrel could dart under and through them very quickly. Soon they could only follow the sound of the squirrel scampering over twigs and dried leaves. And then there was silence.

"We've lost the squirrel," Flora said with a sigh. "We're going to need a new plan." She brushed some leaves off her cape and sat down on a log.

Merryweather plunked down beside her, shivering in her still-wet clothes.

"You're soaked, Merryweather! Let me brew you a cup of hot tea," said Fauna. She lifted her wand to cast a spell. "Oh, dear. I forgot." She stared at her broken wand and sighed.

" Don't lose HOPE ! "

Aurora said to her friends. But as she glanced at the sun sinking low in the sky, her own hope faded. How would they find the squirrel after dusk?

Hoo! Hoo! came the familiar hoot of the owl.

Aurora jumped and covered her heart with her hand. "Oh, Owl, you startled me!" She gazed up at her feathered friend. "Have you by chance seen a squirrel carrying a very, um, *unusual* twig?"

The owl gazed back with wise, round eyes. *Hoo?*

Merryweather stood and put her hands on her hips. "A bothersome thief, that's who!"

As if in response, the owl flapped its wings and took flight. *Hoo! Hoo!*

"I think it wants us to follow!" said Aurora.

She and the fairies tracked the owl through the forest, winding around trees and climbing over logs—deeper and deeper into the woods. As dusk began to fall, shadows crisscrossed their path.

Aurora studied the dark forest, searching for the squirrel. As the wind picked up, branches creaked and groaned. Goose bumps prickled her skin. "I hope we're going the right way," she whispered. "Owl knows where we are. Don't you, Owl?"

The owl swooped low, as if to reassure them that they were on the right path. But when the trail narrowed, Merryweather stopped and took a step backward. She uttered a single word: "Thorns!"

"Where?" asked Aurora.

As if in response, the clouds parted in the night sky. The moon cast a mysterious glow on a snarl of twisted branches covered in prickly thorns.

Flora sucked in her breath. "Those look like the work of . . ."

Hoo? called the owl overhead.

"Maleficent!" spat Merryweather.

Aurora's heart quickened. She had heard of the thicket of

thorns—a trap Maleficent had set for Prince Phillip. The evil fairy had tried to stop the prince from reaching Aurora and breaking the curse placed on her.

As Aurora stared at the briar patch, the thorns seemed to twist and tangle before her very eyes. "But that curse was broken," she whispered. "Those thorns burned up in a blaze of fire. Didn't they?"

Fauna patted Aurora's hand. "That's right, dear." But her eyes darted toward Flora. "They *did* all burn up, didn't they?"

Flora didn't seem so sure. "I think it's best if we avoid the briar patch," she said. "Maleficent's dark magic may still linger in those thorns. They could be poisonous—or hold a curse of their own."

Aurora felt a chill run down her spine. As a cloud drifted over the moon, the thorns took on a greenish glow. Was Flora right? Were those prickly branches filled with Maleficent's dark magic? She shivered and turned away. Then she heard something.

Squeak! Chuck-chuck-chuck. Squeak!

Aurora whirled around and peered deep into the briar patch. She followed the sound toward the twisted branches at the top, where she spotted a trembling squirrel. The wand in its mouth shivered and shook. "It's our squirrel!" Aurora cried.

"With Flora's wand!" said Merryweather. She lunged toward the thorny bushes, but Flora grabbed her cape from behind.

"We can't go in there!" Flora said. "You know the rules of magic. Good fairies can never set foot where evil magic exists."

"But the squirrel looks trapped!" said Fauna. "What if it has fallen under Maleficent's evil spell? We have to help the poor thing."

"And we must get Flora's wand," Merryweather said. "What if we don't and someone else *does*? Someone as evil as Maleficent?"

Aurora shuddered at the thought. As silence fell over the forest, she took a deep breath. And suddenly she knew what she had to do.

"You can't go into the thicket," she said to Merryweather. "Nor can you," she told Fauna. "You heard what Flora said. But maybe *I* can."

"No!" all three fairies said at once.

Their kindness gave Aurora the courage she needed. "Yes," she said firmly. "You saved me from Maleficent's curse once before. Now it's my turn to save you—to save your magic from falling into the wrong hands."

"But what if the thorns are a trap?" asked Fauna, her voice tight with worry.

Aurora swallowed hard and turned back toward the tangled branches. A green mist swirled around them, as if beckoning her forward.

Squeak, squeak! the squirrel cried out again.

Aurora set her jaw. *The squirrel needs my help,* she decided. *And the good fairies do, too.*

"I'll be all right," she said, hoping it was true.

Ever so carefully, she pushed her way through the thorny bushes. As she stepped into the green glow, she sensed a heavy fog settling over her. Her legs felt heavy, and her eyelids began to droop.

Stay awake! she told herself. *Keep going!*

Sharp thorns tangled in her hair and tore at her dress, but she

kept her eyes straight ahead. With every step she took, the prickly branches seemed to wrap themselves more tightly around her.

When she finally reached the squirrel, Aurora blew out her breath. The creature trembled on the branch.

"It's all right," said Aurora in a soothing voice. "I'm here to help you."

As she reached out her hand for the squirrel, it crawled toward her. But thorns suddenly sprouted from all around, blocking the squirrel from taking another step. The squirrel tried to push past the thorns, but the wand in its mouth was too long to allow it through. So the squirrel let go. The wand slid from its mouth and clattered down through the spiny branches.

Aurora's stomach dropped, too. She gasped. Would she be able to find the wand?

The squirrel raced down Aurora's arm and perched on her shoulder, and Fauna cheered. "You saved the squirrel!"

"But what about the wand?" Merryweather cried.

As Aurora knelt to look for the wand, the green fog seemed to grow denser. A sudden wave of sleepiness settled over her. If only she could take a tiny nap. Her eyelids drifted slowly shut. . . .

Chuck-chuck-chuck! the squirrel chattered in her ear, waking her up.

"Do you see the wand?" Flora called.

Aurora peered sleepily through the glowing thicket. The wand rested on a bed of leaves and twigs. She reached carefully through the tangled branches, but the wand was too far away!

"I wish I could bend the branches," she said. "Or perhaps cut through them."

When her sleeve caught on a thorn, her squirrel friend gnawed through the thorny branch, setting her free.

"Oh, what sharp teeth you have!" said Aurora. "Can you chew through a few more branches? Maybe together we could reach the wand."

Chirrup! The squirrel hopped off her shoulder and began gnawing through the brambles.

Aurora stretched her arm through them as far as she could.

Finally her fingertips touched the end of the wand. The squirrel squeaked and scampered back toward her as she gripped the wand firmly in her hand.

Suddenly she heard the crackle of twigs and branches. The thick, gnarly thorns began to wither and shrink, and the green mist faded to gray. Now that the good fairy's wand was back in safe hands, the evil that remained in the thorns vanished. Aurora breathed a sigh of relief as she stood.

With her new friend perched on her shoulder, she made her way out of the thicket and presented Flora with her wand.

"Well done, dear girl!" said Flora. "Thank you!"

"Oh, I do love happy endings!" declared Fauna, wrapping Aurora in a tight hug.

Even Merryweather dabbed at her eyes. Then she cleared her throat. "All right now, back to business. We still have just one wand—not three." She pointed at Fauna's broken wand.

"Oh!" said Flora. "Of course." She waved her wand and, with a shower of sparks, repaired Fauna's. "We'll find yours, too, Merryweather, just as soon as we reach the stream."

"Thank you!" said Fauna, admiring her shiny wand. "It's as good as new. Why, I think it's even better."

As the owl led them to the forest's edge, Flora lit their path with her wand. Fauna admired her new-and-improved wand, hugging it to her heart. Merryweather kept her eyes peeled for the stream. And Aurora breathed in the night air, feeling *very* much awake.

When they reached the stream, Flora sent a glittering trail of magic across the water. It returned moments later, carrying something in its midst.

"My wand!" cried Merryweather.

The squirrel on Aurora's shoulder squeaked and reached for the wand as it passed by.

"Oh, no you don't!" Merryweather scolded. She grabbed her wand just in time.

Aurora laughed. "Time to get you home," she told the squirrel, lifting it toward the hole in the tree. It chattered a sweet goodbye before darting into its nest.

Out of the corner of her eye, Aurora saw Merryweather cast a quick spell. A flurry of soft feathers swirled through the air, straight into the squirrel's nest.

"What are the feathers for?" asked Fauna.

Merryweather shrugged. "Perhaps if its nest is a little more comfortable, that sneaky squirrel won't try stealing our wands again!"

"Merryweather," Aurora whispered. "You *do* care about the squirrel after all."

"Harrumph," said the fairy. With a wave of her wand, she sprouted wings and fluttered off the ground, smiling just a little.

"I'm so pleased that we found all three wands!" said Fauna as they started down the trail.

"We did!" said Aurora. "And all we needed was your special strengths."

"Our special strengths?" asked Flora.

"Why, yes!" said Aurora. "Flora, you're very wise. You came up with a plan for finding the wands. All you needed to do was retrace your steps."

Flora's cheeks turned pink.

"And, Merryweather," Aurora continued, "you're very brave. If you hadn't chased that squirrel, we never would have found its nest!"

Merryweather's mouth twitched into a smile.

"And, Fauna," said Aurora, "you're so kind. If you hadn't been determined to help the squirrel, we never would have retrieved the last wand. You spread kindness everywhere you go."

Fauna dabbed at her eyes. "Well, I do try, dear."

"So you see?" said Aurora. "We didn't need magic to find the wands. All we needed was Flora's wisdom, Merryweather's courage, and Fauna's kindness."

Flora flitted back toward her and smiled. "Someone else showed great wisdom, courage, and kindness tonight, too."

Hoo? called the owl overhead.

"You!" all three fairies said to Aurora.

Aurora's cheeks flushed with pride and happiness. "Well, I did have some help from my forest friends." She looked back at the squirrel's nest and waved at the owl above. For just a moment, she thought she saw a flicker of green in the bushes nearby. But it was only a firefly.

Maleficent's dark magic is gone, she reminded herself. *I'm safe now, and the fairies are, too.*

She turned to follow the three good fairies, who dipped and darted along the trail ahead of her, leading the way home.

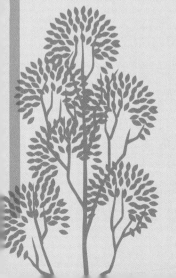

What are your SPECIAL STRENGTHS?

ARIEL

The youngest daughter of King Triton, Ariel loves music, exploring, and above all, the human world. Ariel is fiercely independent. Despite her father's orders never to go above the water's surface, the little mermaid can't help herself. Ariel's unflappable spirit and resilience carry her on a journey of self-discovery, through which she becomes a courageous young woman who discovers her place in the world.

SHINE OF THE SEA

WRITTEN BY ERIC GERON & ILLUSTRATED BY NICOLETTA BALDARI

Ariel burst over a ridge of coral, trying to flip her fins as quickly as she could. She was late for her concert rehearsal—again. Her sisters would be furious—again! She swam even faster, her long red hair blossoming out behind her. Although it was night, the palace shone in front of her, gleaming golden as if lit by the sun.

She heard her sisters before she saw them. Their singing carried through the water to her ears. She followed the sweet sound into the concert hall—a chamber with grand arches and rows of benches. The mermaids were lined up onstage, each of their tails a different color. When they saw her, their singing came to an abrupt stop.

"Look who decided to show up," said Attina, the eldest sister. She narrowed her eyes at Ariel. "What is with you lately?" The other sisters crossed their arms in annoyance.

"I'm sorry, I—" Ariel paused. She wasn't about to tell her sisters the truth: that she'd been distracted ever since the night before, when she'd saved a human sailor from drowning. She shrugged. "I guess I just forgot."

Attina's eyebrows rose. "You forgot? *Again?* Let's hope you don't miss this concert, too."

Ariel winced, recalling how she'd completely missed their last show. Her sisters had been humiliated, and her father had given her a stern talking-to about her "careless behavior."

ARIEL IS . . .

FIERCE
CURIOUS
FREE-SPIRITED
DRIVEN
UNCONVENTIONAL
WILLFUL

ARIEL'S DREAM:

To be part of the human world

HEROIC MOMENT:

Saving a human from drowning

SIDEKICK:

Flounder

FAMOUS QUOTE:

"Have you ever seen anything so wonderful in your entire life?"

"You need to arrive *on time*, dear," Attina continued.

"Yeah," Alana butted in. "Our do-over concert is tonight. Do you even know your part?"

"I-I do," Ariel said, but her shaky voice didn't sound very convincing.

"Great." Attina flashed a sarcastic smile. "Then let's take it from the chorus, sisters!"

The mermaids began to sing again. Ariel let the notes pour from her mouth, clear as a bell, but as she sang, her sisters grew quiet. They swarmed around her, frowning.

"What?" Ariel let out a nervous laugh. "Was I . . . off-key?"

"Ariel, you're supposed to be singing in harmony with us," Attina said. "Your solo comes earlier in the song, which you would know if you weren't always fish-flaking out on rehearsals."

Ariel laced her fingers together. "Please, Attina," she begged. "Let me try again."

"Forget it, Ariel," Attina said. "We don't have time. Our concert's in a few hours."

"But maybe if I only sang my solo—" Ariel began.

Attina chuckled. "So now you get to be late *and* have a say in our arrangement?"

Arista and Aquata giggled, while Andrina, Adella, and Alana averted their eyes.

Ariel fought back tears. "Fine. I won't interfere." And with that, she swam off.

"Ariel, don't be so hasty," Adella called out.

"Come on now, Ariel!"

"Yeah! We're sorry!"

Ariel half-considered turning tail—until she heard Attina's voice: "There goes Ariel acting like a baby again. Come on, girls. We don't need her."

Fists balled at her sides, Ariel torpedoed from the concert hall in an angry stream of bubbles. She was frustrated at herself for letting her sisters down, but she *knew* she could prove she was a team player—if they would only let her.

"Ariel!" Her best friend, Flounder—a yellow fish with blue stripes, fins, and tail—swam after her. "Hey, what's wrong, Ariel?"

"It's my sisters." She sniffled. "They don't want me singing with them."

Flounder blew a raspberry. "I bet they're just jealous of your beautiful voice!"

Ariel gave him a slight smile. "Oh, Flounder. You're the best, but I *was* late to rehearsal."

The little fish sighed. "What can we do to cheer you up?"

Ariel paused before playfully raising an eyebrow. "Follow me!"

"Uh-oh," Flounder said. "I know that look: the one that says you're about to break the rules." He shook his head and pointed his fin back at the concert hall. "Ariel, don't you think we should—"

But Ariel had already swum over the castle's sprawling coral lawns and was now rushing toward the forbidden surface, hoping to distract herself with a glimpse of the sailor she had rescued the night before.

"Hey!" Flounder shouted after her. "Slow down! I'm coming!"

As they rose higher, something overhead caught Ariel's eye. The water's surface was . . . *glowing*?

"What is *that*?" Ariel asked.

Flounder gulped. "M-maybe we don't need to know?"

Ariel broke through the glowing surface into the crisp night air and pushed back her bangs, marveling at how the wave crests were gleaming with rainbow colors. She laughed and twirled, the water shimmering around her. The currents she created churned with a vibrant multicolored light, fizzing in a radiant display. She dipped below the surface and skimmed through the water, which flared around her like a cloak of glowing bubbles.

She surfaced again. "Flounder, isn't this fantastic?!" But it wasn't Flounder who replied.

"Merfolk from Atlantica aren't supposed to visit the surface." A merman had broken through the water beside her. He had coarse short-cropped hair and a warm smile. Behind him bobbed five other unfamiliar merfolk. Each of them had an empty satchel slung over a shoulder.

Ariel was shocked that merfolk other than herself were at the surface, but she was also glad she wasn't the only one who dared swim by her own rules. "I-I was just curious about this glowing." She wasn't about to admit to strangers how frequently she visited the surface. "You're not supposed to be here either, you know."

"It's not forbidden in Pacifica, where we're from," the merman said. He introduced the other merfolk before pointing to himself. "My name's Zeek."

"I'm Ariel, and this scaredy-fish is Flounder," Ariel said as her fish friend peeked out from behind her hair.

Flounder waved sheepishly. "So, do you . . . do you come to the surface often?" he asked Zeek. "You're not afraid?"

"Going to the surface can be very dangerous," Zeek said. "We only come up here when we need something. My friends and I have come a long way to find this brilliant algae bloom." He traced his fingers across the surface, which gleamed iridescent at his touch. "The sea's sparkling with it tonight!"

Ariel's heart swelled—she'd found others who shared her adventurous spirit! "So that's what this is: an algae bloom!" she said, watching a pod of dolphins zip past, their bodies brightening like starlight as they dove through the shimmering water. "I wonder why I've never seen this before."

"Overglow is rare," Zeek said.

"'Overglow'?" Ariel inquired.

"That's what we call it," Zeek said. "It's also known as Shine of the Sea." He grinned. The merfolk were shoving handfuls of overglow into their satchels.

Ariel pointed out the satchels to Flounder. "I wish I'd brought *my* satchel."

Zeek smiled. "There's plenty of overglow to go around."

"Why are you collecting it?" Ariel asked. She noticed that the merfolk were rubbing it into their scales, slicking it through their hair, and streaking it across their lips and eyebrows.

Zeek's features glimmered. "Like it?" he asked.

Ariel somersaulted, elated. "Oh! I love it! You all look radiant!"

"The overglow protects us," Zeek explained. "On the surface, it helps us blend in with the moonlight so we're invisible to any predators below. And when we visit the deep sea, the overglow makes predators think we're toxic to eat."

"The deep sea?" Ariel breathed. "I've never been there."

"You're in luck," Zeek said. "We're about to dive down there to follow the currents to the next kingdom. We'd be happy to give you a tour!"

Ariel's eyes went wide. "Let's go!"

Flounder swam to Ariel's ear and whispered, "I'm not sure that's such a good idea."

Zeek chuckled. "Don't worry, little guy. Just stay close to us and you'll be fine."

One of the mermaids studied Ariel's and Flounder's fins. "But first," she said, "you'll need a little glow-up."

Before Flounder could object, Zeek's mermaid friends surrounded him and Ariel, turning them this way and that in a dizzying swirl of bubbles. When the mermaids backed away, Ariel looked down at herself and gasped.

"It's lovely!" Ariel's entire tail was shining and sparkling! Her fingernails twinkled! Even Flounder's stripes looked more dazzling than ever. Once his eyes stopped rolling around from dizziness, he did a happy little loop-de-loop.

"Now you're ready! Come on!" Zeek plummeted, his friends whooping as they followed.

A smile washed across Ariel's face. Then, with a sinking feeling, she recalled the squabble with her sisters and wished they were as welcoming to her whims as her new friends. Shaking off the thought, she flicked her fins, folded over, and dove after them.

"W-wait for me!" Flounder called.

The water grew darker and colder. Before Ariel knew it, they were down at the ocean floor, a deserted part of the seabed with bleached bone-white coral and wisps of tall black grass.

This couldn't be the "deep sea" Zeek had spoken of. There were few places left in Atlantica she had yet to explore, including the evil sea witch's lair that she'd heard so much about, but she'd already been down to *this* part of the ocean many times. It was nothing new or remarkable. . . .

But then she saw the merfolk slip into a dark fissure running along the ocean floor. She followed them, twisting her body to enter the crack. Inside, she could see it was a trench leading downward.

"Ariel, not to sound like a guppy, b-but I have a bad feeling about this," Flounder said.

But the chance to delve somewhere new filled Ariel's stomach with butterfly fish of excitement. She pumped her fins, eager to explore the unknown.

"Come on, FLOUNDER. There's nothing to fear."

Just then, a huge glowing sea creature reared up out of the dark. "MONSTER!" Flounder screamed. "WE'RE GONNA DIE!"

Ariel spiraled out of its way, slamming back against the trench wall. As Flounder cowered in her hair, she caught her breath, peering down at the horrifying beast. It had long tentacles like a hideous giant squid and large glowing eyes that stared them down. The creature hovered in place, blocking Ariel and Flounder from following the rest of the merfolk down into the trench.

"Zeek! Are you okay?" Ariel called down.

As Zeek emerged into view below, the fearsome glowing sea creature . . . *scattered*? Its menacing eyes and terrifying tentacles seemed to break apart in a flurry of little dots of light.

Ariel blinked hard. It hadn't been a fearsome creature at all, but a group of tiny glowing shrimp. They'd come together to . . . to *scare* her. And it had worked! "Flounder," she said, fishing him out of her hair, "we're okay!"

Zeek gestured to Ariel. "Come on. We're nearly there."

"Y-you mean we're not there yet?" Flounder stammered.

"Is someone getting cold fins?" And with that, Ariel plunged.

Flounder followed. "Ariel, wh-what's that saying about how curiosity killed the catfish?"

"Flounder, will you relax?" she whispered back.

Down, down, down they swam. The trench grew narrower, the water even colder.

Finally, a current spat Ariel out into a dark realm of glowing coral and fish: the deep sea.

"Oh my gosh!" she said, taking it all in. Every creature was aglow—from bobtail squid and comb jellies to dragonfish and lantern sharks—lighting up the dark space like a starry night sky. Her eyes followed a vivid starfish, then a glowing anglerfish. She playfully prodded a jellyfish with tentacles of rainbow lights and got a closer look at tiny fish flashing like lightning. "Have you ever seen anything so amazing?" Ariel asked.

"Uhhh . . ." Flounder replied, but his eyes were wide with wonder.

Zeek and the others made their way through a school of glimmering fish. As she followed the merfolk, Ariel could only make out their overglow-streaked tails, which shone neon in the pitch-dark water. The same went for Flounder, whom she recognized purely from the glow of his distinct stripes, fins, and tail. Her own tail was lit up like magic, along with her fingernails and hair.

"So what do you think?" Zeek asked Ariel.

"I love it!" She gestured at the glittering creatures that swam around them. "Are they all covered in overglow, too?"

Zeek shook his head. "Creatures down here make their own light."

"MONSTER!" Flounder shrieked, darting behind Ariel.

"Flounder, not again—" But Ariel froze. There, at the edge of the trench, appeared a glowing giant squid—not a bunch of shrimp disguised to look like one, but a *real* giant squid. It opened its beak and let out a terrible screech, sending the smaller creatures swimming off to hide among the coral. The hungry giant squid was heading right for Ariel and her friends!

"I-I thought you said the overglow would keep us safe from predators!" Flounder squeaked.

"Stay back," Zeek ordered. He slathered a piece of coral with overglow and tossed it with all his might.

"The squid will go after the decoy," one of the merfolk explained. "Works every time!"

Ariel held her breath as the squid halted and watched the coral drifting past.

But then the squid snapped the coral decoy in half with its beak! It continued toward them, screeching hungrily as it closed in.

"It didn't work!" Ariel cried. "Now what?"

"Glowscreen!" Zeek shouted to his friends, who emptied their satchels so the overglow burst out in a cloud of light. "This will surely distract it. Now swim!" The merfolk turned tail as the monstrous squid got lost in the billow of overglow.

"I think it worked!" Flounder piped up as they followed the merfolk around a corner.

They came to a stop inside a cavern. The merfolk felt along the walls for an exit, but there was no escape.

Zeek whirled around. "It's a dead end!"

"What are we going to do?" squealed Flounder.

"I have an idea!" Ariel exclaimed. Recalling how the shrimp had come together to form a frightening monster, she quickly rounded up the merfolk and gathered them together to create the shape of a large glowing shark. Their luminous fins formed its jagged teeth.

The squid appeared in the cavern's entrance, looming out of the darkness.

Flounder, playing the shark's eye, whimpered. "Ariel, I d-don't think it's w-working!"

The squid spread its massive deadly tentacles and opened its sharp beak, preparing to swallow them whole.

"Flick your fins and don't stop!" Ariel instructed all the merfolk. They did as they were told, making it appear as if their shark was opening its mouth wide and chomping its huge teeth.

The squid recoiled with a shriek—and suddenly retreated. Together, Ariel and her friends had scared it off. Her bright idea had worked!

"That was some quick thinking!" one of the merfolk told Ariel.

"You totally saved our tails!" another agreed.

"It was a team effort!" she replied. If only her sisters had been there to see how well she had worked with others.

"You sure know how to put on a good show, Ariel!" Flounder chimed in.

She gasped. "Oh my gosh! The concert with my sisters! I've gotta go!"

Zeek handed his satchel to Ariel. "Please take this as a parting gift."

She peeked inside. There was still a lot of overglow left. "Oh, thank you, Zeek! But . . . don't you need this to continue on your way through the deep sea?"

"The algae bloom is still up there," he replied. "We can always get more. What's important is that we're able to give back to someone who helped us out."

Ariel beamed. "It was wonderful meeting all of you. I hope our currents cross again someday!" As the other merfolk cheered in agreement, Ariel and Flounder started toward home.

An excited chatter filled the water around the palace. The concert was about to begin. Ariel found her sisters putting on their makeup in the vanity room mirrors.

"Look what the catfish dragged in." Attina glared at her. "Late again, I see."

Arista ran a conch comb through her hair. "At least she didn't leave us high and dry this time!"

"I still can't fathom what was more important than yesterday's concert," Aquata said with a sneer.

Ariel cleared her throat. "I'd . . . I'd like to say something to all of you."

Attina snorted. "This should be good."

"I'm sorry for being late and missing out," Ariel started. "And I promise to sing in harmony so that we all shine together as a team . . . that is, if you'll have me back."

Attina looked at her other sisters.

"I understand if I'm too late and you don't want me to perform with you," Ariel continued. "But even if I'm not singing with you tonight, I wanted to give this to all of you." She opened the satchel to reveal the overglow.

Attina peered inside. "Eww! What is that shiny slime?"

"Overglow." Ariel applied a fresh coat to her lips, eyelids, and hair. Her sisters hovered around, curious. When Ariel snapped her fingers, a huge cloud of tiny shrimp entered the room, gathering around the lights and plunging the room into darkness—just as Ariel had asked them to do.

The sisters gasped.

"Ariel, you're glowing in the dark!" Aquata observed.

"I'm impressed," Attina admitted. "Where'd you get this stuff?"

"That's not important, is it?" Ariel teased. "I knew you'd all like it."

Attina rested a hand on Ariel's shoulder. "We like *you*. And we need *you*. Don't we, girls?"

A little while later, the daughters of Triton took their places inside their clamshells under the stage in the crowded concert hall. After the fanfare from the trumpet fish, and after Sebastian the crab started up the orchestra, King Triton waved his trident so that the stage lights went out, just as Ariel had requested.

Suddenly, the concert hall was as dark as the deep sea itself. Whispers rippled up from the audience.

The orchestra trilled and swelled as the glowing clamshells rose onto the stage. One by one, each clamshell snapped open to reveal a mermaid whose tail and hair were covered in shining streaks of overglow. The last to emerge was Ariel, sparkling green and purple as she let her solo notes bubble out. Then Ariel let her voice slip into

harmony with her sisters as they swam together to form a single glowing rainbow.

When the sisters hit their final, perfect note, the twinkling shrimp floated in right on cue to illuminate the water around them like starlight. The crowd roared with the loudest applause the sisters had ever received.

The concert had gone off swimmingly. It was a performance Ariel would cherish forever as her shining musical debut.

Attina squeezed her hand. "Ariel, we couldn't have lit up the stage without you."

"I promise never to let you down again," Ariel said. Glowing with affection, Ariel pulled her sisters into group a hug. "From now on, we shine together."

How do you HELP others SHINE?

FROZEN
BONUS STORIES

ELSA

Elsa was born with a special gift: the power to create snow and ice. Her power used to make her feel like she didn't belong in the kingdom of Arendelle, and she struggled to understand how to use her magic to help others. But she has learned to accept and love herself—and her power. Elsa now lives in the Enchanted Forest, where she joins the spirits of earth, fire, water, and wind as the Snow Queen.

THE UNHAPPY FOREST

WRITTEN BY SUZANNE FRANCIS & ILLUSTRATED BY NATHANNA ÉRICA

Elsa paused on the forest path and closed her eyes to listen. The creek burbled across smooth stones. A nearby squirrel's nails clicked as it scurried up the rough bark of a tree in search of an acorn. A chorus of birds chirped noisily. But Elsa didn't hear the one thing she was listening for: Bruni, the Fire Spirit.

"Hmmm," Elsa said, opening her eyes. "I wonder where Bruni could be. Any luck, Gale?"

The invisible Wind Spirit whirled over and wrapped around Elsa twice, then zipped upward in search of Bruni. Elsa watched as Gale gently rustled through the arching branches of a tall tree. Dry brown leaves fluttered to the ground while the Wind Spirit wove in and out, trying to find Bruni's hiding place. Then it breezed over a fallen oak, making the tree's branches creak and groan. Giving up, Gale returned to the forest floor, forming into a tiny tornado of dust.

"No sign, huh?" said Elsa.

Gale dashed over and circled Elsa's hands a few times.

"Good idea," Elsa whispered. Then she raised her voice to make sure Bruni could hear her. "I think we should take a break and make a little snow." Elsa knew that Bruni couldn't resist snow. She smiled and waved her hands, calling on her icy magic. "I'll just make a little pile right here."

The Fire Spirit's big eyes peered out from its hiding place inside

ELSA IS . . .

CONFIDENT
WARM
GRACEFUL
POWERFUL
CREATIVE
PROTECTIVE

ELSA'S DREAM:

To keep her family safe

HEROIC MOMENT:

Saving the kingdom of Arendelle
from a flood

SIDEKICK:

Bruni, the Fire Spirit

FAMOUS QUOTE:

"I never knew what I was
capable of."

a moss-covered hollow log. It watched as Elsa created a small mound of fluffy white snow. After a moment, Bruni burst out of the log and leaped into the snow pile. Gale whipped around joyfully.

"Found you!" Elsa said with a laugh. She enjoyed watching the fiery little salamander roll around in the snow, clearly enjoying its cool touch. She sprinkled some snowflakes into the air, and Bruni lapped them up.

Elsa suddenly noticed a distinct shift in the air. She froze in place as an uneasy feeling stirred inside her. She looked down at Bruni, who looked startled. She could tell the Fire Spirit felt out of sorts, too.

"Something isn't right," she said, lowering her hand to the ground. Bruni scampered up into Elsa's palm, and she raised it toward her face. "What is it?" she asked.

Flames ignited on Bruni's back, and Elsa quickly created

a small flurry, attempting to settle the spirit's fire and fear. "Don't worry. We'll figure it out," she said. "We just have to stay calm."

Gale whipped around anxiously, and Elsa knew the Wind Spirit sensed something amiss, too.

The Water Nokk rose out of the creek, appearing beside them in the form of a horse. The Water Spirit shook its mane and pounded its hooves against the forest floor, ready to face whatever was causing the disturbance. Elsa pressed her forehead to its nose, and it seemed to relax a bit. Her touch turned its watery body to ice, and she climbed onto its back.

"Let's go figure out what's wrong," she said to the spirits.

Gale followed and Bruni sat on Elsa's arm as she rode the Water Nokk through the forest. They made a point of checking in on all the forest creatures as they continued down the path. Hawks soared above, beavers chomped at tree trunks, and a few reindeer trotted by. They heard the occasional *tap tap tap* of the woodpeckers knocking on tree bark, searching for bugs. The spirits paused in an open field and watched a few fox cubs wrestling in the tall brown grass.

"All the animals seem happy," said Elsa. "But something just isn't right." She rolled her shoulders, trying to shake off the bad feeling that crept up her spine.

When the group reached the riverbank where the Earth Giants normally slept, they saw that the rocky spirits were wide-awake and restless. The giants shifted, as if trying to get comfortable, causing the earth to tremble slightly. Then they slowly stood and began stomping their feet. Small stones tumbled from their shoulders and splashed into the water.

"We feel it, too," said Elsa, looking up at the Earth Giants. "We're going to figure out what's going on. Just remember to stay calm. We'll fix it together."

Elsa knew the Water Nokk wanted to check on the creatures in the river and sea. She climbed off its back. "Go on," she said. "And let us know if you find anything."

As the spirit disappeared into the water, Elsa looked up at the Earth Giants and said, "We'll signal you if we need you. It will be okay." They nodded and shifted uncomfortably onto their sides in the river.

Bruni sat on Elsa's shoulder and Gale gusted overhead as they wound their way through the forest. It wasn't long before the Fire Spirit jumped down and scampered to inspect a cairn—a small tower made of stacked stones—that had been built next to the path.

"Where did that come from?" asked Elsa. "Perhaps it's a clue."

Bruni scurried ahead and sniffed at another cairn. As they continued through the forest, they saw more little works of art: there were tiny houses made of sticks and leaves, and some small designs scratched into the earth.

Elsa inspected the designs, her senses heightened. She still felt uneasy, but no more so than before. "These are interesting, but I don't think they're causing our discomfort, do you?" She knew the spirits agreed. "There is something else going on."

Just then, they heard a noise. Someone was humming.

They followed the path as it curved around a thick line of oak trees.

Elsa breathed out a sigh of relief. "Olaf!" she said, pleased to see the little snowman.

"Oh, hi, Elsa!" said Olaf. "And hello to you, Bruni!" He grinned as Bruni leaped up onto his twig arm, then scampered across it and onto his snowy head.

"Are you the one who's been leaving the little nature sculptures along the path?" Elsa asked.

Olaf nodded. "I read a book about making art in nature and thought I'd give it a try," he said. "I made rock towers and stick drawings and leaf designs—"

Suddenly, a red squirrel scurried down the side of an oak tree toward Olaf, reaching for his carrot nose. The little snowman dodged him and giggled. "This is my new friend," Olaf told Elsa. "I call him Agnes."

The squirrel tried once again to grab Olaf's nose. He shook his head back and forth, keeping his carrot just out of reach.

"It's a game we've been playing," said Olaf. "Agnes tries to take my nose, and I turn my head to keep it away."

Elsa squinted thoughtfully as she watched the squirrel climb back up the tree. She was certain Olaf's presence in the forest wasn't causing her uneasy feeling, but she wondered about the squirrel's behavior. Why was he so determined to steal Olaf's nose?

"Olaf, have you noticed anything strange going on?" she asked. "There's something creating an imbalance in the forest."

"I don't think so," Olaf replied. "What could this *something* be?"

"That's just it," said Elsa. "We don't know."

"Ooh!" said Olaf. "I love a good mystery. Maybe I can help."

"That would be great," said Elsa.

As the group started down the path, Agnes the squirrel chased them, jumped onto Olaf's shoulder, and once again lunged for his carrot nose.

"Another game?" Olaf said with a giggle, and turned his head to the left. "I win!" The squirrel scampered to his other shoulder, and Olaf turned to the right. "I win again! I'm getting good at this game."

After a few minutes, Elsa noticed that more squirrels were following them down the path.

"Do you guys want to play, too?" Olaf asked the squirrels that were now circling him.

"Uh, Olaf? I'm not sure they're playing," Elsa warned him as the squirrels closed in.

Just then, they heard voices in the distance. The squirrels startled before scampering up into the surrounding trees to hide.

"Hey, guys, where are you going?" Olaf called to the squirrels.

The voices grew louder, and Elsa saw a man and a woman on the trail ahead. The man pulled a small covered cart behind him.

Before Elsa could say anything, Bruni and Gale took off toward the strangers. Bruni's back burst into flames, and Gale whipped through the trees' branches, rattling the leaves.

"Fire!" the man cried as flames suddenly whooshed around them.

"It's the magical spirits!" shouted the woman. "Run!"

"Bruni, stop!" shouted Elsa. She chased after the Fire Spirit, using her ice power to put out the fire before it got out of control. From the corner of her eye, Elsa spotted the strangers running deeper into the woods. They both looked frightened as Bruni and Gale caused windy and fiery chaos around them.

"Please wait!" Elsa called to the strangers. When they didn't stop, Elsa waved her arms to create a sheet of ice beneath their feet, slowing them down. Scared and confused, the strangers clutched

each other for support as they slipped and slid on the ice. The cart slid right along with them.

Gale circled Elsa as she put out Bruni's last fires. "Scaring them isn't going to help," Elsa whispered to the spirits. "We can figure this all out if we stay calm. We just need to speak with them."

The spirits withdrew but stayed on guard, Gale taking the form of an angry dark tornado and Bruni rearing up, all ablaze.

Terrified, the strangers stood still as Elsa approached.

"Please," said Elsa, holding her hands to her heart as a gesture of peace. "We didn't mean to scare you, but we need to talk. Something is happening in the forest, and we think you might know what it's about."

Just then, Olaf appeared, having finally caught up. "Wow, you guys are so fast," he said.

The strangers screamed at the sight of him.

"Is that a talking snowman?" whispered the man.

"I think so?" the woman replied.

"Oh, hello," said Olaf. "I'm Olaf, and I like warm hugs."

The strangers smiled awkwardly, not sure how to react.

"Why don't you have a seat?" Elsa offered. She waved her arms, and the two watched, amazed, as she created an ice bench.

They cautiously sat down, and the woman said, "Thank you. My name's Reina. And this is Magnus."

"Hello," said Magnus, giving a shy wave.

Elsa smiled and introduced herself, Bruni, and Gale. "Can you help us understand why you're here?" she suggested.

"Now that the curse has lifted, we've been coming to explore the forest," Magnus explained.

Elsa nodded. Until recently, an impenetrable mist had shrouded the forest, allowing no one to enter and no one to leave for over thirty years.

"We were happy when we could finally come in and see it," Reina continued. "And it's even more beautiful than we imagined."

Elsa smiled again. "We're happy you're here to enjoy it, but we need to figure out what went wrong."

Gale whipped by the cart, pulling the cover up. Magnus awkwardly tried to keep it down. Elsa peered at the cart curiously.

"We like to forage," explained Reina with a nervous chuckle. "So we were just collecting a few acorns—"

Gale blasted the cover right off the cart, revealing an enormous heap of acorns. The Wind Spirit whirled around the cart excitedly. Bruni scampered to the top of the acorn pile, then looked at Elsa with wide eyes. Right away, Elsa knew that they had discovered the source of the imbalance the spirits had been feeling.

"We thought these acorns might have a little magic in them," Magnus explained. "This being an enchanted forest and all."

"We didn't want to cause any trouble," Reina added. "We were hoping to grow an enchanted forest of our own."

Elsa gently explained that the forest depended on the things it produced to stay balanced. "If too much gets taken, the living things here can suffer," she continued. "Red squirrels, for example, rely on these acorns to help them survive the winter. They spend the entire autumn gathering them up so they will have something to eat in the colder months." She looked at Olaf. "And I think we know at least a few that were on a desperate search for food today."

"Agnes was trying to *eat* my nose?" exclaimed Olaf. He grabbed his carrot to make sure it was still there.

"You may not realize it, but the forest has feelings," Elsa told Magnus and Reina. "It actually misses the acorns you have taken." Then she turned to the spirits. "That's what we were feeling. We knew the forest was sad."

"We're very sorry," said Magnus. Reina nodded in agreement.

Olaf picked up an acorn. "But you were right about one thing," he said. "These things *do* have magic in them."

"I knew it!" said Magnus.

Elsa gestured to the leaves fluttering from the tree branches and said,

"Everything from NATURE is MAGICAL."

Magnus and Reina looked confused.

"True fact," said Olaf. He held up the acorn. "Something this teeny-tiny can grow into *that*!" He pointed up to a towering oak tree nearby. "If that's not magic, I don't know what is."

"Says the talking snowman," Reina said with a smile.

They all gazed up at the tree, admiring it for a quiet moment together. The summer sun made the tree sparkle with silver light.

Gale gently curled through the leaves and branches, causing them to dance and sway.

"We found the acorns in nooks and crannies all over the forest," said Reina. "If we put them all back, will that fix the balance? Will that make the forest happy again?"

Elsa nodded.

"Well," said Magnus, turning to Reina, "we can retrace our steps and return them all. I'll bet we can do it before dark if we start now."

"Let's do it together," Elsa suggested.

Reina and Magnus led the way through the forest as they returned handfuls of acorns to tree hollows and leaf piles. Olaf helped, protectively holding on to his nose while tossing acorns to hungry squirrels that scurried down from the trees.

When the group reached the riverbank, the Water Nokk appeared, rising from the river. Elsa greeted the Water Spirit and introduced it to Magnus and Reina. As she stroked its watery mane, she could tell that the Water Nokk was relaxed and happy, knowing balance was restored.

The Water Spirit joined them as they returned a few more piles of acorns to hidden spots along the river. By the time the cart was empty, the sun was starting to set.

Elsa held her finger to her lips. "Shhh," she said. "Look. The Earth Giants are just waking up from a nap."

A pair of enormous nostrils poked above the river's surface, sending air across the water and causing it to ripple. Reina and Magnus watched, amazed, as one of the giants opened its eyes and looked directly at them.

As the Earth Giant slowly rose out of the water, Gale whipped and whirled around the giant's body. The Earth Giant opened its fist to reveal three smooth rocks in its palm.

Bruni scampered onto the giant's hand, then looked up at the group.

Elsa smiled. "These are for you. Gifts from the forest. With our deepest gratitude."

"Whoa," said Olaf, peering at the rocks. "They're beautiful."

"Go ahead, Olaf," said Elsa. "You do the honors. There's one for each of our guests."

The little snowman picked up the rocks. "One for you," he said, handing one to Reina. "And one for you." He gave one to Magnus. "And one for—Who's this one for?"

Elsa smiled. "For you, Olaf. For helping take care of the forest."

"Me?" said Olaf. Elsa nodded, and the little snowman giggled joyfully. "Thank you, thank you, thank you!" he said. He gave the rock a hug and then looked down at it adoringly. "Aren't you the cutest little rock there ever was?" he said.

Before parting ways, Reina and Magnus thanked Elsa and the spirits. They said they would visit often and vowed always to take care of the forest.

"We won't be bringing our cart again," promised Reina.

"From now on, we will leave only footprints and take only memories," said Magnus.

Elsa and the spirits said goodbye to their new friends and watched them head back down the forest path.

"Look! There's Agnes! Hi, Agnes!" Olaf said.

The squirrel turned and darted toward the little snowman. Olaf

cowered, trying to hide his carrot nose. The squirrel stood up on his hind legs, holding one perfect acorn up to Olaf.

Elsa smiled. "I think Agnes is apologizing."

"Aw, that's so sweet!" Olaf said. He popped the acorn into his mouth and tried to chew. "Thank you, Agnes. It's delicious," he said, though the grimace on his face said otherwise.

Elsa followed Olaf and the spirits back down the path, feeling content and proud. She and the spirits had made the forest happy again, and everything was good and right in the world.

How do
YOUR passions
INSPIRE
others?

ANNA

Anna's greatest gift is her ability to make a personal connection with everyone she meets. Despite her lonely childhood, Anna remained caring and optimistic, leading with her heart and staying true to herself. Whether she's befriending a talking snowman or defending her misunderstood sister, Anna always looks for the best in everyone. Newly crowned as queen of Arendelle, Anna looks forward to giving back to the community she loves.

CLOUDBERRIES FOR A QUEEN

WRITTEN BY SUZANNE FRANCIS & ILLUSTRATED BY ALINA CHAU

Queen Anna of Arendelle pushed her bicycle out in front of the castle and breathed in the fresh air, which smelled of peony blossoms and freshly cut grass.

Summertime had arrived, and it showed in every way. The sky was big and blue, and a bright sun lit the way for long, warm days bursting with outdoor fun.

Ever since she was crowned queen, Anna had been so busy with her royal duties that she'd hardly had a moment to enjoy her favorite outdoor activities. But today she'd made sure to keep her schedule clear so she and Olaf could visit the market together.

"Good morning, Olaf," Anna said as her snowman friend approached. "Ready to head out?" She patted the small platform behind her bicycle seat that she had built especially for him.

Olaf nodded. "But before we go," he said, "there's someone special I want you to meet."

Anna looked around, but didn't see anyone. "Who?"

The little snowman held up his hand and revealed a smooth, speckled rock. "My pet! I named it Rocky." Olaf leaned in and whispered, "I figured a rock was an appropriate starter pet."

"Cute," said Anna.

Olaf held the rock up a bit higher, letting Anna take a closer look. He waited expectantly, looking at her with big eyes. "Don't you want to say hello?" he asked.

ANNA IS . . .

SPIRITED
LOVING
OPTIMISTIC
ENERGETIC
OUTGOING
CARING
DETERMINED

ANNA'S DREAM:

To be surrounded by
friends and love

HEROIC MOMENT:

Choosing to do the next right
thing to save Arendelle and
her sister, Elsa

SIDEKICK:

Olaf

FAMOUS QUOTE:

"I believe in you, more than
anyone. Or anything."

"Um . . ." Anna looked around, feeling self-conscious about talking to a rock. "It's very nice to meet you, Rocky." She awkwardly tapped the rock as if petting a tiny mouse.

Olaf giggled and said, "Rocky's already making friends." He looked down at the rock and whispered to it, "You ride in the front." He reached down and yanked a chunk of nearby grass out of the ground. Then he placed it in the bicycle's basket, making a cozy spot. "There you go," he said, gently setting the rock on top of the bed of grass.

Anna sat on the saddle and planted her foot firmly against the cobblestone to balance. "Okay, Olaf, hop on," she said.

Olaf climbed up to the platform and wiggled back and forth, getting comfortable.

"Ready!" he said, holding on to Anna's waist with his twig arms.

Anna began pedaling toward town, and as she picked up speed,

Olaf let out a long "Ahhhhhhh," enjoying the sound of his voice wobbling along with the bumps in the cobblestone. Anna smiled, remembering when she used to do the same as a little girl. She joined him, and the two sang a chorus of vibrating "ahs" until they arrived at the market.

Anna parked her bike, and Olaf hopped down and leaned toward the basket. "We'll be right back, Rocky," he said. As he and Anna walked toward the market entrance, Olaf whispered, "Rocky's birthday is in a couple of weeks."

Anna nodded. "Really?"

"Yup," said the snowman. "And I want to throw a surprise birthday party. I was hoping you, Kristoff, and Sven would help. We can make paper crowns and delicious food and decorations."

"That sounds great, Olaf. Of course we'll help. I can make *kransekake* if you like."

"Yes!" exclaimed the snowman. "What celebration would be complete without your famous wreath cake? This is going to be the best party ever!"

The two entered the market, where many villagers were chatting as they shopped for groceries. When they saw Anna and Olaf, they fell silent, turned, and bowed, formally greeting their queen.

"Good morning, everyone," said Anna warmly.

"Morning!" sang Olaf.

As Anna and Olaf began shopping, people greeted them with eager smiles and hearty handshakes. Others stood on tiptoe to catch a glimpse of them walking down the aisle.

Olaf leaned over and whispered, "Why is everyone staring at us? Do I have something on my face? Or is something *missing* from my face?" The little snowman reached up and checked his carrot nose to make sure. "Nope. All there. What's going on?"

Anna had noticed that since she had taken her place as queen, the villagers seemed to treat her a little differently. Instead of asking about her day, they dutifully curtsied and bowed. Instead of asking for a helping hand, they offered to do things for *her*.

Anna turned to Olaf and said, "Why don't you go grab the almonds? We'll need them for the kransekake."

"Oh, yes! I *will* grab the almonds," said Olaf. "This is so exciting. The party planning has begun!" he added as he hurried down the next aisle.

When Anna stepped near Mrs. Latham, who was shopping for strawberries, the woman stopped what she was doing and bowed. "Your Majesty," she said.

"Hi, Mrs. Latham!" said Anna cheerfully. "Are you getting ready to make some of your famous fruit soup? I'd love to help you again this summer."

Mrs. Latham thanked Anna, but respectfully declined. "I'm happy to make it myself this year," she said. "It would be an honor to bring it to you at the castle."

"Oh, that's very sweet," said Anna. "But I'll stop by your home for a bowlful whenever it's ready."

As Anna continued shopping, people stopped what they were doing and paused their own conversations to greet her and ask if she needed anything. She missed the vibrant chatter of the townspeople and the sounds of the merchants announcing their daily specials. She wanted to say something to move the attention away from her.

A sly grin crossed her face and she said, "So . . . almost time for the cloudberries. Right?"

The cloudberries.

The very sound of the word put gasps in the air and dreamy expressions on every Arendellian's face.

The Cloudberry Festival was one of Anna's favorite annual traditions. Every summer, everyone in the kingdom journeyed into the woods, armed with baskets. Together, they would search for the golden-yellow berries, gently pulling them from their stems. All day the Arendellians would linger, filling their baskets—and their bellies—until the last berry was picked. Then everyone went home with stained and sticky fingertips, feeling happy and tired. Throughout the days following the event, villagers would share their cloudberry creations—jams, tarts, cakes, and more!—swapping samples and stories of recipe successes and failures.

In a flash, every person at the market was telling cloudberry stories and dreaming of the tart, sweet fruit.

"I heard they're going to be extra sweet this year," said one of the villagers.

"With all the rain we've had, there will be oodles of them," said another. "The woods will be covered!"

As Anna listened, her heart warmed. She felt that sense of connection with the villagers she had been missing, and that made her happy. She could hardly wait the few days until the Cloudberry Festival, when she would get to enjoy her favorite tradition as Arendelle's queen for the first time.

On the morning of the festival, Anna awoke early and rushed around to get ready. She hurried downstairs with her baskets and met Kristoff and his reindeer, Sven, outside.

Kristoff had hooked Sven up to the wagon and they were waiting, ready to go. "There she is," said Kristoff, smiling at Anna. "I knew you wouldn't oversleep for this!"

Anna beamed at him.

"Yay, I'm SO EXCITED!"

"So am I," said Olaf, approaching the group. "And so is Rocky." He jumped into the back of the wagon, carefully cupping his twig hands around his pet rock. "You haven't forgotten about Rocky's surprise party, have you?" he whispered to Anna.

"Of course not!" Anna said, though if she was being honest, she hadn't been able to think about anything but the Cloudberry Festival since market day. "We'll start planning as soon as we get back to the castle."

"All right, Sven," said Kristoff as Anna and Olaf settled in next to him. "Let's go!" Sven pulled the wagon and the friends rode toward the bridge.

Anna looked around at the empty streets. "It's so quiet," she said. "Are we early? Are we going to be the first ones there?"

Kristoff shrugged. "Doesn't seem that early," he said.

As they continued, there was still no one in sight. "Where is everyone?" asked Anna. She gasped. "Are we late? No. Was it yesterday? No. What's going on?"

Kristoff laughed. "Deep breaths," he said. "Maybe everyone got there early? I don't know, but we'll find out soon enough. It's not a very long trip."

When the group made it into the woods, Kristoff pulled the wagon over. They grabbed their baskets and eagerly climbed out.

"I don't get it," said Anna, walking ahead. "It's never this quiet. . . ." Anna led the group down a slender, curving path. They turned a corner to an open field and gasped at the sight before them: all the villagers smiling proudly and standing beside a smorgasbord of cloudberries and cloudberry treats. There were cloudberry tarts, candies, and jars of jam wrapped in beautiful bows alongside bowls of cloudberries and cream and pitchers of cloudberry juice.

"Surprise!" the villagers shouted.

Olaf held up his rock and whispered, "I don't think we are going to pick berries today, Rocky."

Mrs. Latham presented Anna with a tray of cloudberry tarts dusted with sparkling sugar. "We picked every berry at its perfect ripeness and prepared them all as a gift for our beloved queen!"

"We wanted your first cloudberry season as queen to be extra special!" said another villager.

"Extra special for our extra special queen!" shouted another.

"To Queen Anna of Arendelle!" they cheered.

Anna took in the expressions of pride on the villagers' faces. "I don't know what to say," she started. "I'm so moved by this surprise. Thank you."

She thanked Mrs. Latham again as she took a tart from the tray. But as she tasted her first delicious bite, she couldn't help feeling a little sad. Even so, she kept a smile on her face while the villagers continued to offer her the treats they had prepared.

When they returned to the castle, Kristoff took Anna's hand. "I know you were excited to pick the berries," he said.

"Their surprise was so thoughtful," started Anna. "But—"

"You missed the experience. That's part of the fun," Kristoff said. "I get it. I enjoy pulling ice out of the fjord myself and would be disappointed if someone did it for me." He wrapped Anna in a hug.

Anna wondered if he was right. Was that what she was feeling? Sadness over not picking berries? She couldn't put her finger on it. She felt so grateful . . . but why did she also feel disappointed?

"They had the best of intentions," added Kristoff. "They did it because they love you so much."

Anna knew this was true. "Things have been different between the villagers and me, and I've been trying to fix it, but—" She let out a sigh. "Well, I guess I haven't."

"You'll figure it out," said Kristoff. "You always do."

She grinned, grateful for Kristoff's encouragement. Then a realization hit. "Oh, but now I have to wait another whole *year* before I can pick a berry!" she said.

"Is that so?" Kristoff asked with a sly smile. He reached into his pocket and pulled out a small green sprig. A perfect amber cloudberry dangled from its end. "I don't know how they missed it. It only took me a couple hours to find," he said with a laugh. "I know it's not the same, but it's the best I could do. Go ahead."

"Awww, Kristoff," said Anna. She plucked the berry off its stem

and popped it into her mouth. "Thank you," she said, giving him a hug.

Over the next few days, Anna was so busy with her royal duties, she hardly had a moment to think. When she wasn't writing decrees or fielding requests from the villagers, she helped Olaf prepare for Rocky's surprise birthday party. Together with Kristoff and Sven, they came up with ideas for the celebration, and Olaf wrote out a list to stay organized. Then they spent time together making paper crowns, decorations, and confetti. She enjoyed the planning so much that she almost forgot about how lonely she'd felt after the Cloudberry Festival.

But every time Anna left the castle, she was reminded how much her relationships with the villagers had changed since she became queen.

Before she was queen, Mr. Hylton would often ask her to help him find his lost false teeth, but these days, she noticed that his daughter followed him around everywhere, making sure they stayed in his mouth.

She used to help Ms. Blodgett with her bread deliveries. They would have so much fun, racing to bring warm bread to the villagers. But lately, Ms. Blodgett insisted on doing the deliveries herself.

And whenever Anna went by the schoolhouse, no students ever seemed to need her to tutor them.

As happy and honored as Anna was to be queen, part of her missed the way things used to be. It was almost as if the villagers saw "Queen Anna" as someone different: someone who was not "Anna" anymore. She feared the distance between her and the villagers was growing, and she knew she had to do something to fix it.

On the day of Rocky's surprise party, Olaf helped Anna decorate the kransekake, drizzling frosting onto each ring-shaped cookie and stacking them until they made a perfect tower. After Olaf placed the final cookie on top, the two carried it into the dining room, where Kristoff and Sven were waiting. Kristoff loaded confetti into the confetti cannon, and the group put up the decorations they had made. Finally, they looked around the room, pleased with the festive atmosphere they'd created together.

"Okay, everyone," Olaf said. "Put on your crowns and hide. I'll go get Rocky."

Anna and Kristoff shared a smile and hid behind the curtains while Sven barely managed to squeeze himself under the table.

When Olaf returned, the group jumped out and yelled, "Surprise!" Kristoff set off the confetti cannon and colorful bits of paper blasted through the air.

"Your throne," said Olaf as he placed the rock onto a small bed of soft, green grass he had set up on the table. Then he put the tiny crown on top of the rock and sang, "Happy birthday, Rocky!"

The group cheered and looked at the guest of honor sitting motionless on the table.

Then Olaf turned to his friends and said, "Thanks, guys. That was fun!"

Anna and Kristoff exchanged a confused look. "Is the party over?" asked Kristoff.

"Rocky's just a rock, remember?" the little snowman said with a giggle. "The real fun was planning the party with you guys. Working together to make all this." He gestured at the colorful room. "*That* was the best part."

"It was fun," said Anna. She thought about Olaf's words for a moment. "Planning the party and working together *was* the fun part . . . wasn't it?" She turned to Kristoff. "I think that's what I've been missing. The fun of working *alongside* the villagers." She gave Olaf a warm hug. "Thank you, Olaf. You're the best!"

The next day, Anna went out and talked to the villagers. She found Mrs. Latham and said, "I really enjoyed helping you make fruit soup last summer. Can we do it again this year?"

Mrs. Latham paused before saying, "I would be more than happy to make some for you today and bring it over to the castle."

Anna explained that she enjoyed being with Mrs. Latham and making the soup together. "I like spending time with you in your kitchen," she added. "Besides, your fruit soup is always delicious— but it tastes even better in your company."

A smile spread across Mrs. Latham's face. She and Anna set a date for fruit-soup making.

Anna found Mr. Hylton and his daughter next. She reminded him how much fun they had searching for his teeth. "It was like a treasure hunt, and I miss how we'd work together to solve the mystery!" she said. Soon enough, Mr. Hylton promised to tell Anna the next time he lost his teeth—and his daughter promised to let them go missing every once in a while.

Anna went to the bakery and told Ms. Blodgett that she missed racing around in the morning, helping her with her bread deliveries.

"Nothing beats the smell of your fresh bread, and I love seeing the joy on your face when people take their first bite."

Anna continued talking to different villagers, explaining how she had been missing working alongside them the way they had before she was queen. And in the following months, Anna and the villagers grew closer as they enjoyed working together again. It became clear to all of Arendelle that Anna wanted to be a different kind of queen: one who stood beside them, not apart from them.

The following summer, as the cloudberries ripened and the festival approached, Anna felt a distinct change in the air. On the day of the festival, with all of Arendelle gathered in the woods, every juicy berry was still waiting to be picked when Anna arrived with her basket.

"We would like to honor our queen," Mrs. Latham announced, "by inviting her to pick the very first cloudberry!"

The villagers cheered.

"And we expect her to fill that basket," said Mr. Hylton.

"And have stains on her fingers by the end of the day!" added Ms. Blodgett.

"Thank you so much," said Anna, delighted.

For the rest of the day, Anna enjoyed laughing, chatting, searching, and picking cloudberries alongside the people of Arendelle. She could tell the distance between her and the villagers had been replaced by a new togetherness. "Queen Anna of Arendelle" was still "Anna"—and Arendelle loved her for it.

What kind of
LEADER
will YOU be?

Printed in the United States of America

First Hardcover Edition, October 2021
1 3 5 7 9 10 8 6 4 2
FAC-034274-21232

Library of Congress Control Number: 2021937369
ISBN 978-1-368-07711-8

Designed by Scott Piehl and Margie Peng

Visit www.disneybooks.com